I changed th
judge, jury, a
No one!

To anyone looking in, we were just a normal church going, family. No one was aware of the dark secrets we held within the walls of the tiny house by the swamp.

I was the woman with the razor strop and I made sure every blow connected.

That was until the day the sheriff handed me my subpoena. I felt the hair stand up on the back of my neck. Abuse? What? The one-word ringing in my head drowning out anything and everything else that might have been said. I felt I might just pass out right there on the step. I kept my composure until he pulled out of the driveway and then my anger quickly exploded into rage.

Those ungrateful little bastards. After everything, I did for them. This was my thanks.

A bolt of straight adrenaline shot through my veins and I grabbed the gun…..

I had instilled the fear of god in them. I am not a woman to be tampered with. How could this be happening?

My one mistake…and I don't make many… was not realizing that these stupid children would grow up.

ROSIE CHRISTIE

As Tears Go By
Copyright © 2016 by Rosie Christie

This novel is Fiction – Based on True Events.
Parts of the storyline are fictional.
Any similarities to any persons or event are entirely coincidental.
The abuse suffered by these children, on a daily basis, is a true and accurate reporting and covers a twelve-year period.

Names and identifying characteristics have been changed.

ISBN 978-0-9952607-0-2 (pbk)
ISBN 978-0-9952607-1-9 (e-book)

Printed by Createspace.com

DEDICATION

For Nicole, Natasha and Lucas, my two beautiful daughters and my very handsome grandson. I have been gifted with not one, but three of the most important people in my world. There were many factors that pulled us apart and it was forgiveness and understanding that brought us back together. There are no words to express the way I feel but I do know that without you I am lost. I am hoping that writing this book will explain some of my actions.

ACKNOWLEDGMENTS

My daughters, Nicole and Natasha, who stood by me through all my complicated and not always healthy life choices.

My sisters, Sharon and Darlene who are always there, always supportive, always inspiring and always my sisters. I don't think there has ever been a closer bond.

I can't forget all the rest of my family and friends who have stood by me and encouraged me since the very first day I announced, "I am an Author".

I would like to thank my friend, Marg, and my daughter Nicole, for reading and rereading my manuscript, giving me suggestions and keeping me on track. I would like to thank Joanne, Jill, Judy, and Allysa for reading and providing critical feedback, Ahmed for assisting with my cover pages, and my sister Sharon for her editing skills.

I would also like to acknowledge Joel Osteen, and Joyce Meyers, who inspire me daily and have helped me to learn to forgive and try to deal with everything I have been through. They have also played a crucial role in me becoming a born again Christian.

And my constant companion, my savior, the great God All Mighty, who sees all, protects, and provides comfort. I know I would not be here today without him.

1 MARIA

'Maria..., Maria...' I heard faintly in the distance. I scanned the shoreline, squinting, trying to determine where it was coming from, and then turned quickly, losing my footing briefly, before wading back to shore. I noticed the bottom of my skirt was damp where it had fallen in the water and I squeezed out the excess as I bent down to grab my moccasins. Heading back to the pow-wow I couldn't help stopping to admire the scenery. So peaceful. So beautiful. Barely dusk and the sky above the tree line lit up like an amber fire. I must be hearing things I thought as I shook my head but as I turned I heard it again.

'Maria..., Maria... ' came whispering through the trees. An eerie sound, not quite human. It was emitting from all directions, rippling the leaves in its journey with a force so intense that even Mother Nature was unable to protect her tiny leaves as they were ripped from the branches. And as it passed, I watched the leaves float gently down to blanket the earth below, unaware of the disruption. There was a familiarity about it and even as quiet as a whisper, it coursed through me, determined to brand an imprint there for eternity. I raced back to the ceremony, slipping my moccasins on as I ran.

Squeezing my way through the crowd I stopped. I heard nothing now and I felt safe. Then I saw the light. It was coming for me. I tried to scream but my vocal cords were lost, severed in my throat. My legs seemed to extend roots and the blood churning through my veins turned to ice. The tightening in my chest was unbearable and I gasped for air waiting in anticipation for its next move.

I glanced frantically around the crowd but everyone was intent on the ceremony. They had to have heard it I thought but the drummers continued to drum even louder. A crowd this large, and I was all alone. I turned back as the light swooped down, Dancing and swirling around my feet. I squirmed frantically trying to escape its touch, knowing it was evil. Twirling faster and faster I tried to escape.

A claustrophobic effect washed over me, and then as the light engulfed me, it tightened around my body so tightly I couldn't catch my breath. The lights were memorizing and then when I felt I could take it no longer, it released its hold and I fell to the ground. I bolted upright, soaked in sweat only to gaze tearfully around my bedroom. I snuggled deeper into the warmth of the old worn out mattress, pulling my quilted blanket tightly against my face, until the bile in my throat, subsided. It was a dream. Just a dream. It always left me feeling drained, weak, and scared. That and the two-four Gary and I had polished off last night accounted for the bad taste in my mouth. I'd had the dream before and as if by omen, bad luck followed.

Mulling over what happened the night before I remembered sitting with Gary and the children after work. Dinner had been great and then somewhere through the evening Gary and I had decided to have a few drinks. I caught only glimpses and pieces as the night progressed, Gary and I had started fighting, again. My most vivid memory, standing in the bathroom washing the blood off of my face. It always ended the same. I wanted so much more from our relationship. A family as I'd always dreamed of it. Husband, wife and beautiful children.

Well, I had the beautiful children. Unfortunately, it was I that shattered the rest of my dream. Gary begged me to marry him over and over through the years but I heeded my Father's wishes from many years before,

"If you marry a white man, you and my future grandchildren, will lose your native status."

So even though my heart said yes, my head said no. That didn't stop us from producing three perfect children, in addition to my son from a previous marriage.

Gary couldn't understand my refusal to marry him. I knew I should discuss it with him but even after all these years, it was still too sensitive a subject to broach. I had been married the day I left residential school. The dreams had started there. Each dream going just one step further than the last.

I had been so happy to leave the school that I referred to as home for more than a decade. At fourteen, I was oblivious to the fact that I was leaving one nightmare to enter another. It was a tearful reunion as my father appeared to collect me. Mistaking my tears for happiness, he was distant and aloof. Never an emotional man, he wasn't prepared to handle the situation. I couldn't tell him that my tears were a subtle display of helplessness. My baby brother, David, would not be accompanying us. I had to leave him at their mercy. I'll never forget those feelings of helplessness. It was worse than any hell I had endured at their hands. It tormented me for many years until I saw David again. He too had survived.

Upon leaving the school, my father drove me directly to a small church where I would meet and marry my first husband. An ugly, mean man, and that's all I'll say. The only good thing from that union was my son, Johnny. At sixteen, I'd had enough and with Johnny strapped in a moss bag on my back, we hit the road. I stuck my thumb out and let it take us where it would. This would be our first trip to Montana. The most beautiful place in the world.

We left our native traditions behind and attempted to fit into a white man's world. As luck would have it I spotted a Help Wanted Sign almost immediately. I was unaware that day that I would meet a family that would touch my life. I was leery entering the restaurant with Johnny but I knew of no other way. My fears were unfounded. The owner produced a piece of candy and pushed it into Johnny's pudgy outstretched hand as his wife scurried from the kitchen to greet us.   Walter and his wife, Andrea displayed a genuine warmth towards us and the feelings were mutual. As I worked as a waitress in their restaurant, their teenage daughter Cindy watched Johnny, in a small room above the restaurant that they had converted into an apartment. It wasn't roomy but it was a place for my son and I to call home. We became a part of the Anderson family. Two years later, when the business started to falter, it was Walter that came to me, tears glistening in his eyes, to tell me that they would have to let me go. It wasn't a complete shock. The business had really dwindled since the buffet opened, down the street. Again I followed my thumb and the long journey eventually brought us back to the great plains of Alberta.

It would be several years later while visiting in

Calgary, that I would meet Gary. I had left Johnny with my father and I was attempting to secure a job. Jobs were scarce though and I wasn't having much luck. Drinking one night, in one of the not so desirable bars, I noticed one of the bouncers trying to get my attention. He was continually walking by, flirting, buying me drinks. Finally, I stopped him, persuaded him to sit with me and we started to chat. His name was Scott and he wasn't making a lot of money. We talked until the wee hours of the morning and by the next night, I was working. We had it all worked out. I'd target one of the guys. Once they were drunk, I'd slip their wallet out of their pocket and toss it to Scott. Scott would take the money out and send it sailing back. Once it was back in their pocket, I'd make my get away. Scott and I split the money at the end of each night. I didn't feel it was wrong, merely survival.

It was on one of my busier nights, I'd already cleared out about four wallets when one of the guys became irate as he watched his wallet go sailing over to Scott. In addition to having one too many, I was so confident now, I'd let my guard down. I was on the floor nursing a fat lip before I knew what had hit me. I wasn't even aware that the same guy had made a lunge for Scott. The bar transpired into a brawl around me and I sat dumbfounded until someone held a hand out to help me off of the floor. I looked up into the warmest eyes before I was quickly hustled out of harm's way.

That was my first meeting of Gary. It didn't take long for him to persuade me to leave Scott and we landed a couple of jobs in a lumber camp. Five years of hard labor in the brush land and our love continued to flourish. I had finally met my life's mate. In coming to this conclusion, Dolly was conceived. And then, in rapid succession, Jacob joined her, and two years later, baby Rayen. Two boys, two girls. My pride and joy.

Our relationship was a roller-coaster of good times and bad. We drank too much now and then, but overall, we were blessed with a happy, healthy family. Gary was a good, kind man and proved to be a wonderful father both to Johnny, Jacob, and our daughters. He was attentive and he became fluent in Cree. Unable to avoid the pitfalls of any relationship, ours too had struggled on numerous occasions throughout the years. The latest, was the most troubling, catching Gary in bed with Brenda, an eighteen-year-old from Onion Lake. Gary and I had been working such long hours, and we'd brought her in to take care of the children. I had noticed things were changing. Subtle changes at first but I felt threatened. I was devastated walking in on them, a month ago. I had twisted my ankle at work and arrived home earlier than expected. I cursed myself for not reacting to my strong feelings earlier. Gary assured me it meant nothing and went out of his way to convince me of his love. He told me repeatedly how sorry he was. I wasn't sure if he was sorry for doing it, or just sorry for getting caught. A few days elapsed and after much discussion, we decided that we would put it behind us. But try as I might, I couldn't rid the horrid picture. It kept playing over and over in my mind. When Gary held me, did he think of the way he held Brenda? When he kissed me, did he imagine he was kissing her? I was going crazy. It was transforming me into this vindictive crazy woman that I didn't know. Once the children were asleep, the night was mine. To ease my pain, I settled down with a companion of whiskey and so alas, last night had proved to be no different.

My lips were rough and as I licked them, the salty taste of dried blood filled my mouth. Well, Gary could pick up his cheque today and we'd go over to the reserve store and pick up groceries. I vaguely remembered the baby crying last night. I'd stumbled around in the dark for a few minutes and finally fell back into bed. She had quieted down. Dolly must have gotten up. She's such a darling. Always so helpful. Even at five.

Leaving, for some reason, that word kept popping into my head. Did Gary say he was leaving? I vaguely remembered talking to him early this morning. He had been preoccupied the last while and wanted to take the children to his mother in Ontario. He was so concerned that our children would be taken to residential school like me. There was no way in hell I would ever let that happen. We would go hide in the mountains and live off the land. Gary would take care of us. He was just talking foolishly.

As bad as I felt I pulled myself to an upright position on the bed. I felt his side of the bed but it was cold. I'd have to get the children ready and go look for him. Hopefully, it wasn't at the bar. How long had I slept? Minutes, hours. It felt more like days.

As much as we fight, he is the father of my children and I love him. And we only really fight when we drink. We'd just have to quit.

"Dolly," I yelled. My voice echoed through the tiny three-room shack, sending stabbing pain through my head. The house was quiet.

"Jacob," I yelled again. Nothing.

I rushed out to wake the children. The tiny room the children shared was empty. The beds unmade, clothes strewn all over the floor. A mess made from packing in a hurry. The whole house was empty.

For the first time in six years, I panicked. The type of panic to which your heart drops to the pit of your stomach and sends the blood careening through your veins out of control. I dressed quickly, oblivious to the fact that it was Gary's shirt I put on and pushed my feet into my moccasins. Struggling, my feet swollen from the alcohol, refusing to fit I pressed harder. I was wasting precious time. Finally, barefoot, I threw open the door and hobbled out. Where could he be? The train station.

I could see the building from where I stood. In contrast to the other buildings on the reserve that were old and run-down, it stood out like a sore thumb. Erected last year by the railway company, it was painted brightly in reds and blues. Definitely not of our tradition. The band members had fought to keep it off the land but reconsidered when the price of the claim increased too significantly to ignore. There would be a railway stop in Thunderchild. The men had been here for weeks, hammering and making a heck of a racket. In the end, the building stood tall, the train stopping daily. Normally this made no difference to me. I was happy in my little home. Food, shelter, and love were all I needed to survive but now it seemed that this too may be falling apart.

He's won't leave. He's trying to scare me. Well, it worked. I was scared. I had to catch him. I'd just let him know that I'd quit drinking and make sure he did too. It was as simple as that. We had tried hard to quit drinking a few months back when the kids were taken away to a foster home in Edmonton. During the four months the children were gone I attended alcohol treatment. Gary found a job in Hinton, Alberta and we planned to move to Hinton. I finally agreed to marry him and we would be a family again. It would be wonderful. The final six days waiting to see the judge had seemed more like an eternity.

Gary and I vowed that we would work harder to keep our family together. Everything had been going smoothly until this Brenda thing. I never needed any help before. I don't know what had possessed me to let her into my home. Let her into my bed. I was upset. Anybody would be. Now Gary was playing this cruel joke.

As I entered the dimly lit train station I spotted Gary and the children sitting on the solitary bench. I was annoyed yet relieved. The words tumbling out of my mouth before I reached them. "O.K. Gary, come home. You've made your point. I won't mention Brenda again. I promise. We'll just forget it."

Gary's head hung, his eyes glued to the floor.

I dropped down on the floor so that he would have to look at me. He didn't look well. "I'll quit drinking, Gary. You too. We'll do it together. You're acting crazy. I'm their mother. I can do this."

Gary didn't answer.

"We have to go, Maria." He finally said quietly. "We've tried and tried. Neither of us can quit drinking. We say it but we don't. It's not fair to the kids. They'll be better off with my mom for a while. Your father told me the government men were by the house again. They are taking children. You know what those schools are like Maria. I have seen what they have done to you. You have never gotten over it. I know that's why you can't quit drinking. I don't want them to take the kids. Once I'm settled and we have a place to live I'll come get you. I have to do this."

I heard the train squealing to a stop in front of the station. I had to convince Gary quickly that I was serious.

Frantically words started spewing out of my mouth.

"Those government men can go to hell. I don't care about them. We can do this. Please Gary please, please, please. We can go to meetings, sweats, whatever it takes. Even if you don't want to stop drinking, I will. For the children. I'll do anything for my children. We can move away from here. Start over." I knew I was rambling. "Don't do this."

"Maria, how many times have we been over this?"

Behind us, the conductor began yelling "Boarding, boarding," like there were a lot of people around or something. It was so annoying.

"Not enough times." I pleaded. "Come home, honey, and we'll talk this over where it's quiet."

Gary shook his head. "Come on," I begged.

"Maria, I said no. You know we only got the kids back a short time ago with the condition that we would take them to my mother in Ontario. I thought we could make it work as a family Maria and I know you have tried. You say you'll quit. You go for treatment and then you fall off again. I love you Maria but we have to go."

"How long have you been planning this?"

"I have been speaking to your father about it for a few weeks, now and I decided last night it was time."

"You decided," I said angrily.

"Yes, I decided. I decided when Rayen was crying and she needed her mother and you were too drunk to go to her. That's when I decided."

He started herding the children towards the exit and handing tickets to the conductor. I stood frozen unable to respond. He turned at the door. "Kids, give your mother a hug. We have to go."

Dolly was on his far side but managed to slip past him before Jacob. She slid her little arms around my neck, squeezing me so tightly, I was sure I'd choke. "I don't want to go Mommy. I want to stay here with you."

"Oh Dolly, I want that too." I could hardly see her through my tears. The other children started to cry.

"Maria, don't make it harder on the kids. You two, get over here. Give your mother a kiss. We'll see her again soon."

Gary pulled Dolly away and the baby was in my arms. I held her tight, drinking in her sweet baby smell, I kissed her forehead and then I did the only thing I could possibly think of. I bolted for the door with her in my arms. I took the stairs two at a time and raced for the train tracks. I ran faster than I thought was humanly possible. I had covered a fair distance when my foot caught on something and I felt myself falling. I wrapped my body around Rayen, protecting her as we rolled and eventually landed hard on the ground.

By the time I had regained my composure Gary had caught up with us and had Rayen in his arms. I watched the back of him as he took long strides back towards the train. I pulled myself to my feet. As I put pressure on my foot excruciating pain shot up my leg. Ignoring the pain I hobbled as quickly as I could to catch up with them.

This had to be a nightmare. This wasn't real. I would wake up in a few minutes, nursing a hang-over. The children running rampant through the house but as the pain became more unbearable I knew it wasn't a dream.

"Gary, I beg you, don't do this. They're my babies." I yelled as I made my way up to the train platform.

I only got a glimpse of the kids with Gary inside the train. Dolly was peeking shyly at me under his arm waving bye, bye, unaware of what was happening. I didn't see Jacob. I hadn't even gotten to hug him. I did catch a glimpse of him for a brief moment as the door slammed shut.

"I'm sorry, Maria." Was all I heard.

The engine was getting louder and I knew it was ready to pull away. This wasn't a dream. I ran to the door, banging on it with my fists, the glass quivering under the impact.

"Gary, Come back."

Gary's dark hair appeared at one of the windows.

"Where's Johnny?" I screamed.

"Your fathers. He's at your fathers..."

The train started picking up speed. I ran after it crying and yelling. Dolly and Jacob both started banging their little fists on the window too.

"No," I screamed chasing them. "No." As the train disappeared from sight.

The pain in my heart was so heavy. The pain in my leg so debilitating that I collapsed in a heap.

Hours later, I finally pulled my weary body off the tracks. I had stayed there, praying another train would come by and stop my pain. Questions racing through my mind, over and over. Why wasn't I able to stop him? I had the baby I should have run home. What was I thinking?

Finally, it dawned on me. Gary won't go through with this. He'll get to the first town and turn around and come back. He just trying to teach me a lesson. As I came to this revelation, my heart beat slowed down dramatically.

I'd go home, clean the house and make supper. They'd be starving by the time they got back. I hummed a tune as I made my way back home. A gospel tune I'd learned in residential school. I shuddered as the song brought back a flood of memories and decided to walk faster instead.

I wanted everything to be perfect. I stopped at the entrance, surveying the largest room in the house. A living room, kitchen combined. Looking at it through the eyes of a stranger, I was able to drink in every detail. The paint peeling from the ceiling, the stains running down the walls. Every day I walked through here but I never really noticed it. This was probably true of my husband and my children as well. When they got home things would really change. I started here, scrubbing diligently until the stains and most of the paint came off. Content with the results, I turned my attention to the bedroom Gary and I share. The solitude window in our room was covered with a dull white curtain, ripped on the one side that made it hang down in a grotesque sort of way. I pulled it off and replaced it with a clean towel. That looked better. Hanging up the clothes, I spotted an unfinished drink under the chair in the corner. I brought it to my lips and savored the sweet smell. And with the temptation so great, I ran to the door and heaved it as far as I could throw it. Not able to pull my glance away I watched as it sailed through the air, smashing into an old abandoned car, beside the creek. The liquid steaming, as it disappeared into the earth, returning to its place of origin. I was proud when I returned and spread the blanket across the mattress on the floor before moving on to the kid's room. We had boarded up the children's windows last winter when it was so cold. Gary and I had dreamed of building a huge house with a bedroom for everyone. A five bedroom house that we could call home. It hadn't happened yet but up to this point it hadn't seemed like a priority. Now it was. The double bed that Dolly and Rayen shared against the children's far wall ate up most of the room and I noticed how dark it was in here. How bleak that must appear to the children. I'd make them a new quilt. There was a huge pile of old clothes in the cupboard that I was saving for a rainy day. That day was here. If I used all the pretty colors in the box, it would brighten up the room tremendously. I made a mental note to have Gary take the boards off the window as soon as he got home. Jacob's twin mattress was just about new. My brother David had dropped it off when he heard me mention that we needed a bed for Jacob.

Even though the house was small I had gone through it painstakingly slow. It had been more than two hours since I started cleaning. I'd have to start dinner quick or it wouldn't be ready when they got home. There weren't many groceries but I proceeded to prepare a feast. I killed one of the chickens. It wasn't quite old enough but I was sure Gary wouldn't mind. I cleaned it and stuffed it with the last of the bread. The garden still had an abundance of potatoes that I peeled with vigor. Bannock, just the way he liked it. Flowers. I grabbed a jar from under the sink and practically skipped across the road to the field. There were wildflowers coloring the field in multiple colors and an aroma that was strong and sweet. With the flowers displayed in the middle of the table, everything was perfect. I surveyed the room and was satisfied with the results. Then I sat down to wait.

My hands had a visible shake so I clenched them tightly together on my lap. A drink sure would take the edge off. I hadn't realized the full impact of my hangover until now. I could do this. I could get through anything as long as I had Gary and my kids. And I didn't want anything to jeopardize our reunion. Just give him an excuse to pull another stunt like today. I smiled satisfactorily.

As I sat there, I smelt a putrid smell. Peering cautiously around the room, I came to the conclusion that it was me. My god, I must look like death warmed over. I'd been so caught up in everything that was going on that I hadn't bothered about myself. I wandered out to the woodshed, only to discover Gary had let it go empty. Figures, but I wouldn't let it annoy me with so much work still to be done. I was totally invigorated by the time I'd finished chopping a couple armfuls of wood. It felt good to leave my frustrations at the wood block. With the water boiling on the old wood stove, I dragged the wash tub across the floor. Cup after cup of hot scalding water slid slowly over my head. I was enjoying this brief holiday of solitude. It wasn't until my breasts began to ache, heavy with milk that my thoughts again returned to the children. My baby must be hungry. The little one I lovingly referred to as, bright eyes or sparkling eyes. This pushed me into action and I scrambled from the tub, dressing quickly. I wanted to be ready when they came home.

The minutes dragged on like hours. This time of year

the gophers were busy trying to stock their nests for the winter. Even so, every time I heard so much as a twig snap, I raced to the door. By nine o'clock I turned off the dried up chicken and went to sit on the steps. I grabbed Gary's thick blue sweater on the way out. It was hanging by the door. He must have forgotten it. It smelt slightly musky and I wrapped it tightly around me wishing it was him. I was totally unaware that my shaking was a result of lack of nutrition, shock and the need for a drink. As midnight approached, I moved back into the living room, sitting on the couch with my knees under my chin.

I was determined to be right there when everyone came home. I was in this same position when I woke in the morning. The pain in my breasts unbearable. I squeezed them releasing the milk that was causing my torment and then stopped, basking in the pain I knew I must endure for my sins.

Days turned to weeks as I checked the train station faithfully, fully expected to see Gary and my children standing on the platform. Johnny and I spent afternoons waiting and praying. As the days passed I wanted nothing more than the comfort and warmth of my whole family together once more. Johnny, inclined to be a quiet lad, thrived on my attention. He was all I had now and I was determined to be the best mother possible for him.

The evenings were the hardest. It meant another day without my children. In the bedroom, Johnny would crawl up beside me on my bed. "Mommy, don't cry, Mommy," he'd say, which only managed to make me cry harder. Other times he'd question me about his brother and sisters. Where were they? When would they come back? Difficult questions that even I couldn't answer. Running my fingers through his long dark hair, I'd hold him close and rock him until he fell asleep. He was so young. Too young to understand.

With Johnny asleep, I'd proceed to the children's

15

room. It had become a nightly ritual. I needed to tuck the girl's dolls into their bed too. It was the only thing right now that was keeping my sanity. Dolly's old doll that my mother had made for her before she'd passed away. The one that no longer had a face that she refused to sleep without. Did she miss her doll as much as I missed her? Jacob's blanket, so worn that the stitching was all but missing that he had trailed behind him faithfully, rain or shine. There were times when I had to pull it out of his clenched little fist as he slept so I could wash it. Now I refused to wash it until he returned. And the babies bottle that I cradled in my arms, before the yearning in my heart became too much and I cried myself to sleep with the one and only picture I had, held tightly in my hand.

Some nights I would just lay in bed remembering all the good times we had. Piling the kids into the wagon to go get water from the creek was always an adventure. Dolly, Johnny, and Jacob would all try to sit as far back in the wagon as possible so they wouldn't get their feet wet as Gary backed the wagon into the creek but it was inevitable that we would all come home soaked. Gary would playfully throw a handful of water first and then the fight was on. I never had a fair chance because I would be one handed splashing with Rayen in my arm. I could still hear them all giggling. Our good times far outweighed any bad memories. How had everything gone so wrong?

In the months that followed, I continued to ask myself, how a man that loved me for more than a decade, could do this. I couldn't comprehend it. I frantically searched the recesses of my mind, the crevices forgotten with time, attempting to restore any recollection that might assist me in the search for my children. This man I'd called my husband. This man I knew so little about. He grew up in Ontario, but I didn't know where. He left home because of some unspeakable act he'd committed, but I didn't know what.

On one hand, there were so many things he didn't understand about me. The winter when my brother David was unemployed and he, his wife and his two children had come to live with us, here in our tiny house. Gary couldn't understand that. When I gave away the good dress he had bought me, to my niece. He couldn't understand that. In a world that places a monetary value on everything, he didn't understand that I didn't need material things. I only needed his love. That was our way. The way of our people.

But then, on the other hand, he knew me oh so well. I had gone for alcohol treatment in Edmonton when the children were apprehended. I tried. I tried so hard but I had failed. No one could ever understand the torment I went through each and every day because of that cursed school. The memories were always there and I tried to push them down and I tried to push them away. They always came back to haunt me. I would smell a smell, hear a song, the sound of a baby cry and all the memories would overwhelm me to the point I could hardly function.

Gary, if you hear me, and I'm sure you can. You must feel my pain. Bring my children home. They need their mother, and I need them.

And then, as the cold realization kicked in. I hated him. I hated him for leaving. I hated him for drinking. I hated him for creating this void that had swallowed up my children. This aching void that could never be filled until he brought them back. A black hole unattainable to me. And even as I thought of him with disgust, my body ached for him. Yearning for him to hold me. His body hard from years of heavy lifting, lying next to mine. Everything as it had been before. And as the emptiness filled my heart, the bleakness in my eyes and the tears spilling over, burnt imprints on my face. I hated myself. I hated that I drank. I hated that I went to residential school. I hated that I wasn't strong enough to be the mother and wife that I wanted to be. I hated everything. Gary knew me oh so well. He couldn't control me so instead he did what he thought was his only other recourse. He had won. He had succeeded for now. He had broken my spirit.

Was he right? The courts had given his mother temporary custody and the thought of my girls being raised in those cursed residential schools was terrifying. Did they have those schools in Ontario? Ontario, in my mind, was at least a half a world away. Oh Creator, please hear my prayers…keep them safe……bring my children home.

2 KATE

"Shut up." I said, "I am going to give it to you straight. You are nothing to me. I don't want you, or your sister, and I won't listen to you cry." I hissed. "If you make another noise I will knock you into next week. Do you understand?"

Jacob looked blankly into my face. What a stupid child. I pulled him roughly to his feet and marched him upstairs.

"This is where you will sleep. This is not your room. You do not own anything in my house."

I turned quickly and started back down the stairs. I was about halfway down when I heard him cry. I turned around and straight back up I went. I glared at him as I entered the room. He was standing right where I had left him. Between the two beds in the middle of the small room. I grabbed him by the arm, half carrying, and half dragging and threw him on the bed. I turned him over and smacked him as hard as I could. I had only hit him a couple times when I heard an approaching car. "Shut up, if I hear you crying, you'll get it again and I ran quickly back downstairs to greet my children and my husband, Victor. This was the end of my life as I once knew it.

If I hadn't been dreaming about Gary in the outhouse and nearly burnt the house down, if I had managed to snag Gary years ago before he took off out west and if Victor and Gary's mother had not just croaked. If, if, if. Well, it wasn't doing me a bit of good now.

As my family came into the kitchen, I sat down at the table and sighed.

"Ok sit down, we need to talk." Victor pulled a chair up at the head of the table and my beautiful girls each grabbed a chair. Of course, they had to fight over the same one. I wasn't looking forward to this one bit. I paused for a moment to catch my breath and then continued.

"I don't know if daddy told you yet but he has decided that Jacob and his sister, Rayen will come and live with us." I made sure I emphasized the word, he.

"Why mom?" my eldest girl Sally piped up. Matilda just sat at the table smiling.

"Well, they need a place to stay and your father has decided, so Jacob will sleep in Matilda's room and Matilda will have to move over into your room with you Sally. I glanced at Victor hoping he would say something but he didn't say anything just sat there smiling like an idiot.

Sally and Matilda started talking at once and I had no idea what either of them were saying. It was just giving me a damn headache. I clapped my hands to get their attention.

"Hey, hey, hey. This is what your father has decided so we must make the most of it. I'm so sorry girls but we will have more money now and mommy and daddy can buy you nice things ok." This seemed to work because they immediately quieted down.

"It's nearly time for bed. Sally take Matilda upstairs and help her take as much of her stuff as she can to your room. Just set it on the floor and we'll deal with it tomorrow."

Sally was sitting with her arms crossed with a frown that dimpled her forehead. "I'm moving to grandma's house."

Finally, Victor spoke up, "No, you're not, Sally. It is a bit of an adjustment but you're a big girl. You can do this for daddy, right?"

"Ok, daddy but I don't like it. Not one bit." And she stomped upstairs loudly, yelling back down, "I hate them already." She banged her door shut loud enough to wake up the baby so I went back to get her. Matilda followed. She was four-year-old and she was my baby girl.

She watched as I changed and fed the baby and then I went upstairs to tuck her in as well.

"Don't stay up too late girls." As I walked out of what was now Sally and Matilda's room.

"Why can't Matilda stay in Jacob's room?" Sally asked. "She's annoying."

"Jacob is a boy so he needs to have his own room and you two girls will have to share. It's not fair but that's what your father wants."

I started slowly down the stairs. I felt terrible that my girls were being put through all this agony because of those kids.

So this is what my life had resorted to. I flopped down on the couch.

Seven years it had been since Victor and I moved out of Edna and Stan's, his parents. The memories were so vivid. Even after all these years Victor never suspected I was in love with his brother.

I had loved Gary since the first moment I laid eyes on him. I was six or seven. We were all swinging on a rope and falling into the river. One by one we would take our

21

turn and as we got close to shore Gary would reach out, hold our hand and pull us back onto the shore. It was from that very moment that I knew Gary would be my husband.

I drifted back to the very last time I saw him before he took off out west. I'd never forget it. He had that James Dean haircut and those tight jeans. He should have been a movie star. And then just like that, he was gone.

Ah, Victor, what to say. My husband totally opposite of Gary. I'm not sure now what had attracted me to him. Maybe it was that haunted look in his eyes. Timid and shy. He did everything I ever asked him to do, and he was there.

It was me that had gone to him that night. It was me that instigated everything. Right down to the sneaking into Bradshaw's store to swipe the 6 bottle of liquor. I was so scared I would get caught but I was determined to get pregnant. How naive I had been thinking that I would get away from this god forsaken hick town. I really believed that one of them would take me away. To a big city and I didn't even care where. But Gary screwed all that up. He pissed off out west. I would have gone with him if he asked. But no, he hooked up with some squaw out there and I was stuck with his brother.

I didn't even like thinking about when Victor found out I was pregnant. Our mother's had decided everything for us. I knew he'd do the right thing and within months we were married. Mother had insisted I be married before I gave birth. I should have followed Gary out west. I should have told him I was pregnant with his child.

Well, it was much too late for any of that. And now after all these years I was expected to raise his little heathens. Maybe it is just as well that I ended up with Victor. Victor has a weakness in his demeanor that works nicely for me. Gary was so headstrong and all.

I still didn't know what exactly happened that night. I'm sure I slept with both of them, but that night was such a blur. That old abandoned bus. So many people. What a party. I had never drank so much in my life. OMG, I was sick for days. As soon as I found out I was pregnant I knew it was Gary's baby. I was getting excited just thinking about him. The warm feeling in my groin was exciting me and I felt a flush creep into my cheeks.

Victor was still upset with his mother's passing. Had it only been three days? Meddling old fool. By the time she had finally gone to the doctor the lung cancer was late into progression. That old bitch. She had done everything to break us up. She had even called me a whore. I wasn't sorry to see her go. Gary had shown up a few months ago, right out of the blue with those filthy half-breeds. They had been staying at his mother's.

Three sniveling stink'n brats! Somebody should have drowned them in the lake like unwanted puppies. I could do that. Pack them in the car and put them in little bags and throw them in the lake with rocks to weigh them down. I smiled.

Well, at least I only got stuck with two of them and not three. I was rudely interrupted by Victor.

He looked tired, "How are the kids?

"Oh, they are just fine," I said. |If you're going to bed don't wake Rayen ok. She's in a laundry basket in our room."

"I'll be quiet Kate." He said. "Don't stay up too late." As he took off down the hall to the bedroom. He didn't have too far go, our house is pretty small. It was adequate for us when we were a family of four but now with six we needed a bigger one. We had scraped and scrounged to get enough money to buy this land. It wasn't my first choice but it was affordable and I wasn't about to spend another night at his mother's house. Living with them after we'd been married had been sheer hell. The measly six months living there seemed more like a decade. It was a large piece of land, at least an acre and when I first laid eyes on it, it was all swamp.

I had said to Victor, "How in hell are we going to build a house here?"

The house took longer to build than the actual clearing of the land. Victor had assured me that his brothers would help us clear it. And believe me, he had enough brothers. His mother had been a regular baby machine which resulted in seven brothers and three sisters. I couldn't really talk, though, my mom had outdone her with a total of twelve in our family. Six brothers and six sisters. So between the two families, we had a small army. We had worked night and day to clear the land. We always went home cold and wet but eventually the stage came where the trucks could come in and dump gravel and dirt. And the trucks came. They brought truck load after truck load, alternating the gravel and dirt and gradually the big void was filled and leveled. It was easier work for me now because I didn't have to do it. For one thing, I didn't know what I was doing and the second reason was because I was progressing quickly in my pregnancy and had started showing. Or at least that was my excuse.

The final result was a modest house with three bedrooms, two upstairs and one on the main floor, a sewing room, living room, kitchen and a place for a bathroom. Once we had the furniture and appliances in the house it had come to life. The house was white with blue trim around the windows and the door.

Victor had planted a small tree off to the right of the yard and we had planted grass seed. It hadn't taken long and the yard seemed to come to life as well. Once we got settled in I planted a few flower beds along the sidewalk leading up to the house and placed white painted rocks around it to create a border. Looking from the road, the entrance to our house was on the left side and lead directly into the kitchen. The living room was direct to the right, at the front of the house and if you walked straight ahead you passed my sitting room. If you continued on, our bedroom was to the right and directly ahead of that Victor had built a room for a bathroom. The plumbing didn't exist yet but there was a white pail that we used at night. We had run out of money. During the day we had to venture out to the back of the yard where the outhouse had been clumsily erected. The house structure was circular and if you went walked through the living room you would confront a coat closet that connected to my bedroom closet. Up the stairs were my girl's bedrooms. It wasn't a mansion but it was mine and I didn't have to share it with a zillion siblings. It hadn't changed much in seven years.

Now everything was ruined. Victor's family didn't want me to be happy. They hated me and they tricked me into taking these stupid kids.

I went in and crawled into bed beside Victor.

I was so tired from the last few days with the funeral and all the goings on. As tired as I was the last few days played back in my head like a movie.

The wake, Edna lying in her casket in the living room. So many people sad and crying. To me, it was no different than when I took the sling-shot and took the heads off of those squirrels. Pesky, annoying and dead.

A lot of people went in to see her but I had nothing to say to her so I stayed back out of the way acting like the perfect daughter-in-law. They had a nice house. The living room was the finest of all the rooms with heavy cabinets and mirrors so your worship could admire herself. The walls were papered with plush velvet swirls and the green shag carpet had been raked to perfection.

The room reeked of beauty. Stan had worked long hard hours in the mill to make sure that he spoiled Edna with the finest that money could buy. He worshiped her and she had let him work himself to death. No one ever really saw much of Stan. Even the short time we lived with Edna and Stan I had only seen him briefly. He had passed away two years ago in September. It was a nightmare after he passed away Edna had nothing better to do than try to break up relationships.

It still pissed me off with our modest income, we had paid so much for her coffin. Victor didn't make much working as a painter and all the boys had chipped in and paid an exorbitant amount of money for Edna's casket. It was polished oak .They got it in Peterborough I think. It was beautiful but then they just put it in the ground. What a waste.

My girls looked so pretty that day. Sally was the oldest. At seven, she stood fairly tall with long dark straight hair. She resembled Victor a little but she looked more like me. It had taken me a long time to get pregnant again but eventually Matilda was born. My baby, Matilda was already four. The only thing that really bothered me that day was when Matilda said. "Mommy, is Grandma all gone? Sally told me that grandma is all gone and she is not coming back".

Tears had welled up in her little eyes and I had reached down and picked her. I hugged her close and said, "Yes darling, Grandma went to Heaven to be with Grandpa".

Then, she peed her pants and we had to come home.

I knew that day someone would have to take those brats but I sure didn't expect it to be me. I had toyed with the idea of offering to take them just to see Gary on a regular basis but I didn't want them.

Gary had no work when he returned to Ontario only those filthy half-breeds and they had moved straight into his mother's house. I adjusted the blankets to cover my feet. Sure I had taken a quick look at them when I was over at Edna's months back but we weren't on the best speaking terms so there wasn't a lot of chance to see them anyway. The only reason I had gone over in the first place was to try and speak to Gary but he wasn't there. Probably at the Arlington, our one, and only hotel, unless he had changed dramatically since I had seen him last.

A thunderous snore erupted from the other side of the bed. I jumped and then realized what had disturbed me. With caution, I drifted back and collected my thoughts again.

I remembered hearing some noise emitting from Edna's living room and curiosity had gotten the best of me and I quietly peeked in.

Two of the children were sitting in an oversized chair. The boy on the chair had long brown hair and was attempting to calm down his little sister. The little sister was like a butterball. She had a mound of curly brown hair and big brown eyes. She was saying some strange words that I couldn't understand as English. Someone was taking their pictures. I can't remember who it was.

Then I noticed the older child. She was standing so quietly that I didn't notice her at first. She had the blackest hair I had ever seen. She was staring out the window. She looked about five-years-old.

Edna had appeared around the corner and startled me. I remember feeling guilty that she caught me looking at them but I tossed this away with a shrug of my shoulder and said dryly. "Oh hi, Edna".

"Beautiful children aren't they," she said. "Three little angels. I am going to take care of them until Gary can get on his feet."

Her tone changed then and she continued. "You stay away from him. I've seen you watching him you little hussy. It's bad enough that Victor is stuck with you. I don't want you corrupting any more of my family. You put my poor Stan in his grave. God rest his soul."

I glared at her and went out and slammed the door. Can you imagine the nerve of that old battle axe accusing me of killing her husband? No, she did that all by herself.

Sitting in the car I saw Laura came traipsing out of the house all smiles. God, I hated that bitch.

As I lay there I felt the frustration from that moment all over again even though it had happened months ago. Like Gary would ever get on his feet. Well maybe not on his feet, maybe on his back and then we can continue where we finished off. I laughed to myself and with this happy thought I rolled over.

Peter's wife Linda had talked to me briefly the night of the wake. She had said that her and Peter would like to take the oldest girl Dolly. I had brushed her off as quickly as I could and made my way outside to get away from them all.

It was like she already knew then that I would be stuck with these two.

With that, I adjusted my pillow again and fell into a restless sleep. I envisioned all the children from the town coming to live in our little house. I awoke in a panic.

The sun was shining through the bedroom window. I reached over for Victor but the bed was empty. I could smell coffee brewing. When I walked into the kitchen the children were already there and Victor had fixed them some oatmeal for breakfast. I mumbled a good morning and headed back to my bedroom.

About a week later Mrs.White called me and I hoped no one was listening in. We had a party line that means two other neighbors have the same phone line as us and depending on the sound of the ring then the appropriate person is supposed to answer it. Sometimes I listen in just to get the gossip. If you are very quiet no one knows you're there.

Mrs.White said. "Kate, I don't know what to do. After we picked up Dolly from Peter and Linda's she cried all the way home. I expected her to be upset but I don't know what to do with her. She cries constantly and she won't eat anything. I even took her to see Father Ginelli to see if he could suggest anything."

With this Mrs.White started to cry. I tried to comfort her but I honestly had no suggestions. My mind was blank. I had enough problem of my own.

The elderly woman continued. "I am doing the best I can but if this keeps up we're going to have to make other arrangements. Bob and I are getting too old."

With that, we both hung up. Oh, Great. I thought. I am definitely speaking to Victor when he comes home. I won't be responsible for yet another child. Why didn't Peter and Linda take her? I would have to ask Victor.

Victor came home that night and we were so preoccupied doing laundry and getting groceries that I didn't bother him to tell him what Mrs. White had said. I also omitted the fact that I had received two cheques in the mail that day. The envelopes were brown and the return address read Ontario Children's Aid Society. The monthly cheques combined surpassed Victor's measly income. It can wait I thought.

Maybe we could keep the kids for a while. Just long enough to put in indoor plumbing and a few other things that we needed. The kids didn't actually cost us much more. Yah, this could work.

I woke up to the sound of a baby crying. At first, I thought I was dreaming. Then I felt someone shaking my shoulder gently.

Victor said. "Kate, There's the baby. She must be hungry."

The baby was just a little over a year old and Victor

and I had decided to keep her in our bedroom. At least until she got a little bit older. Right now I was glad that we had made that decision. I was so tired my eyes felt like they had lead weights on both lids.

"Yah, yah. I'll get her."

I pulled myself slowly out of bed, reached down to pick up the baby and padded into the kitchen.

Thank god I had prepared a bottle for bed. With the baby positioned on one hip, I pulled the bottle out of the fridge and placed a small pot from the bottom cupboard on the stove. I stood there feeling the warmth from the burner and waited until it boiled. When I saw the first few bubbles I put the bottle in.

With this done, I sat down at the table and lit up. A shiver ran through me from the drafts in the kitchen. The baby sat quietly on my lap looking around. She babbled once in a while. By the time I'd finished my cigarette, the bottle was warm. I squirted a few drops of milk on the inside of my arm to make sure it wasn't too hot. Then I took a quick look to make sure my cigarette was completely out and moved quickly down the hall. Baby intact. Back to the warmth of the bedroom. I crawled back into bed, cradling the baby in my arms.

I had stayed up many a night with my own girls and I was too tired to have to put up with somebody else's. I placed her back into her bed and practically jumped the two feet back to our bed. Victor stirred as I interrupted his sleep but his body was like a furnace and I snuggled up close. It seemed like I had barely gotten back to bed and the alarm started blaring loudly.

Victor jumped up. I was a little slower to respond.

After rummaging through the closet I found my housecoat and put on my slippers. I emerged from the bedroom a few minutes later to make breakfast.

As Victor was eating the eggs and bacon, I had prepared, he said. "How are things going honey? I hope the extra kids aren't too much work."

"No Victor," I replied "Everything is fine. Don't worry about it."

I wouldn't let them become more work. Jacob was old enough to help out. Of course, the baby couldn't do much right now but give her time. As I hustled him out the door to catch his ride I said, "Don't worry about us, the kids and I are just going to take it easy today." The car was just starting to back out of the driveway and I spotted Victor's lunch on the kitchen cupboard. I grabbed it and lunged out the door. Pajamas and all. I was thankful that I had at least put on a house coat and slippers. Victor spotted me and the car pulled to a stop. Victor rolled down the window as I approached and I leaned in with his lunch. I gave him a quick peck on the cheek, turned and ran full throttle back to the house. I heard him yell. "See you tonight." When I reentered the house it still had a chill and I hoped I would warm up quickly. Just what I need. I thought now with my luck I'll catch my death of pneumonia.

The children got up shortly after Victor left and I scurried around the kitchen preparing breakfast. Well, Puffs would have to do. I pulled out bowls and spoons and quickly put them on the table. I was in a great mood today considering Rayen had kept me up all night. The children all ate and Jacob was the lone body at the table. As I turned back around from the sink I saw his cup go flying across the table. Milk flowed like a little stream across my hardwood table.

Clumsy, clumsy idiot.

I walked over and said. "Did you do that?"

Jacob didn't answer. He kept his head down.

I asked you something. Now answer me."

Again there was no response.

I gritted my teeth and grabbed him. Before I knew what had happened he had a large red mark on his cheek, from the back of my hand. Shit. I thought.

"The next time I tell you to answer me you better do it. You will obey me."

With this, I marched him upstairs to his bedroom.

"You will stay here until Victor comes home. I better not see you again."

I stomped back downstairs to tend to my girls. My children played in the living room all afternoon. They were perfect angels. I was blessed with quiet loving children. They took turns holding and playing with the baby. I even enjoyed playing with the baby.

About an hour before Victor came home, he usually comes home shortly after 5:00 I ran upstairs. Jacob was asleep. I checked him quickly to see if there were any marks left on his face but they had faded. I woke him up and said. "You can come downstairs now." He had a frightened look on his face but he followed me to the stairs.

I turned around as we got there and leaned down to her ear and whispered. "If you ever tell Victor anything that happens here with me or if you ever tell him I've made you cry. I will kill you. And don't think I'm kidding, because I will. Do you understand?"

He nodded his head.

"Good. Now that that's settled. Come on downstairs."

I walked down the stairs ahead of him and he followed slowly behind. As I walked through the living room the children were playing a game of jacks and I continued to the kitchen to finish preparing supper.

By the time Victor came home all the children were playing happily together.

3 MARIA

It had been two long painful months since my kids had boarded the train with their father. During that brief period I had written letters to Gary begging him to send for me like he had promised or to come back but with nowhere to send them, the envelopes sat blank on the table. A constant reminder as I walked by them each day of the helplessness I felt.

Last week my sister, Gwen's children were picked up. She had been cooking at a feast and left in the early morning hours. She arrived home around dinner time to find her babysitter bewildered, confused and crying. I was shocked when she arrived at my door. She didn't even have to tell me what had happened. I knew from her swollen eyes.

She ran straight into my arms and I held her as she sobbed. "I wasn't able to say goodbye, Maria. They're gone." I held her close as she continued sobbing. "My babies are gone, they're really gone." I had no words of wisdom for my sister so I was silent. At least I was able to say goodbye.

Her Susie was four-years-old. Susie and my Jacob shared the same birth month. Susie's older brother John was five-years-old. Gwen and I had been pregnant together that year as well. My heart ached not only for my children but also my nieces and nephews. Gwen and I knew how her children would be treated, what they were in for. We could only pray that the schools were somehow better. It was like a slap in the face when I realized that Rayen still a baby and she was too young to go to school. She should still be home with me. Dammit Gary.

I considered packing Johnny up and heading into the mountains with him but I was torn. If Gary and my girls came back they wouldn't find us. I also knew if we were caught without a pass off of the reserve it would mean jail for me and then what would become of Johnny. So we stayed. We decided that if the men came to take Johnny to school that he was to run to my father's and hide in the shed until I came for him. I hadn't really thought it through completely or formulated a plan for after that but it was something.

I awoke abruptly in a cold sweat. I had the dream again. This time, it had progressed even further than ever before. This time, no longer how hard I struggled the light would not let go and I was suffocating. I felt the bile creeping up my throat. I fought desperately only to awake with my handmade blanket clenched tightly in my fists, drenched with sweat. My night table was overturned and my heart was racing. Why was I plagued with this reoccurring nightmare? I would get tobacco today and speak to one of the elders. I prayed and smudged and finally, my heart resumed its normal beat.

I had no sooner finished making breakfast for Johnny and there was a knock at the door. When I peered out the window I saw a big black car that I didn't recognize. I grabbed Johnny's hand and pointed with my lips towards his room. With lightning speed, we raced to his bedroom careful as to not make a sound. I grabbed his gray sweater off his bed and threw it over his shoulder raising the window. Johnny's feet had barely touched the ground and I heard him kicking and screaming. "Leave him alone," I screamed as a suited man dragged him to a waiting car. The seconds that it took me to get to the front door felt like forever. I threw the door open but he was gone.

I ran as fast as I could to my brother, David's house but I knew even before I reached the house that it was too late. I could hear my brother's wife wailing as I approached the house. They were both outside. My brother sitting on the ground with his head in his hands. His wife walking around in circles crying.

I walked over with my arms wide and she walked right into them. I held her and we cried. My mind raising, why can't they just leave us alone? We just want to be mothers. We need our families. None of this made any sense. Why are they treating our people like this? My brother stood up and without a word he walked away, down the road.

The whole reserve was falling apart and gradually all of our children disappeared. There was still a handful of babies living sporadically throughout the town site but the normal laughter from the playground was replaced with a silence so deafening that it made the reserve seem eerie.

All of this change triggered so many memories of my childhood. It all came flooding back and with it all the bleak and unspeakable things that had happened. It was at times like this that I was relieved my girls and Jacob were with their father and not stuck at the mercy of the residential schools. It all seemed so hopeless. I wanted my children back.

I had lots of time to think now. Way more hours in the day than I cared to have. Memories of my drinking made me feel ashamed. I had been drinking before Gary took the kids but not all the time. Sometimes my thoughts were so dark I needed the drinks to make them go away. I never in my wildest dream envisioned any of this happening.

I still felt a disconnectedness from my family. I had a compassion and love only for my brother David. Mainly because we were at the same residential school together. Even though we could never talk I did see him on the other side of the fence. He was my only connection to what I referred to as, my real world. The world before residential school. My other siblings were older so they had been taken earlier than David and I. They were sent to different schools. It wouldn't have mattered anyway because siblings were not allowed to talk, touch or spend any time together. When we finally united together with our father so many years had passed that we seemed no more than strangers. They were my family and I loved them but we were not a family anymore.

After they took our children I watched helplessly by, as my brother David sank deeper and deeper into depression. He seemed to take it harder than most and was drinking extremely heavy. Johnny was gone now so I had no one to care for, or tuck in, or love for that matter. This just made me cry harder missing all my children and cursing anyone that would listen. I had a consuming anger that would not leave no matter how hard I tried. I began to drink with David and days gradually turned into weeks. Sometimes other people from the reserve came to drink with us and most times it was just him and me. I liked when it was just the two of us. I enjoyed just sharing the silence with him. We never talked about the school but it loomed over us like a plague that never, ever went away. We had all been there. We all knew what was in store for our children. How had things become so terribly wrong? How could the Creator let this happen?

I finally sobered up and went to see my father. He told me to come stay with him. With Johnny gone we were both lonely and it made sense. As angry as I was, I continued to pray to the Creator every night. I smudged and I prayed for a sign. I had to believe that he would protect and blanket my girls, Jacob and Johnny with the strength they would need to keep them safe until we were all together again. My heart ached each day but I refused to give up hope.

My father got an off-reserve pass so we could take the journey to Battleford. It took over a week but it was finally approved and we planned our trip.

It finally came to me, the name, Maynooth. It was Maynooth Ontario. I had been trying and trying to remember where Gary had said he was raised. I ran to my house, grabbed the letters off of the table. Quickly scribbled Gary's name and underneath I wrote Maynooth, Ontario. It was all that I had. I shoved it in my pocket and raced off. Father was waiting.

I was thankful for the fall weather. It was neither too hot nor too cold. It was so beautiful but I had no time to enjoy the surroundings. My only thought was to get help to get my children. It seemed like our journey would never end but eventually, we pulled up to the small building. I was confident that the RCMP would be able to help me and I started to squirm in the wagon. It had been such a long trip and I knew I must look disheveled but regardless I was excited, determined and scared. When the wagon stopped I didn't move.

"Maria", my father said. "We have come a long way." I nodded, took a deep breath and made my way to the door.

I pulled the heavy door open and as I entered the

strong smell of tobacco and urine made me gag. I stood in the doorway and let my eyes become accustomed to the dark room. I was startled when I heard a gruff voice. "What are you doing in here?" With a soft voice, I said. "I need help to find my children."

"Speak up" he barked at me.

"I am trying to get help to find my children," I said a little louder.

"Are you drunk?" Under his breath, I heard him mutter, "great another drunk". I despised him immediately.

"No, I am not drunk." I walked quickly to the counter but I wanted to turn tail and run.

Another man stepped out of an office. A little office in the back that I hadn't noticed right away. I felt claustrophobic as memories of residential school overwhelmed me. I couldn't breathe and I took a step back. 'What's going on?" The new man asked. The two men standing behind the desk both looked huge.

"Oh, we have a drunk looking for her kids. Probably forgot where she left them." The first man said and then they both laughed like he had made some funny joke.

This made my blood boil and I said. "I am NOT drunk. I have 3 children who were taken from me by their father. Two daughters and my son and I need help to get them back.

"Go home. Go back to the reserve. We can't help you."

With that said, the first man came quickly around the desk and pushed me forcibly towards the door.

I lost my footing for a brief moment and then I turned and ran. As the door banged shut behind me I cried. I wasn't in pain. I cried with frustration and anger. I wiped my tears roughly away and jumped back on the wagon. Without a word, my father pulled away. I didn't have to tell him. He knew.

It was hopeless.

For some reason, the Creator was punishing me and I had no idea what I had done wrong. All the way home I prayed for forgiveness. I tried to console myself with the knowledge that my kids were not in residential school. I think the schools are harder on girls but maybe I was only being biased. David never spoke of what had happened to him. I know he continued to have nightmares as well. The one night we were drinking I woke up to a blood-curdling scream that scared me half to death. I ran to shake David who was passed out on the couch. He was thrashing around and when he was finally conscious he rose quickly and went into the other room so I wouldn't see him wiping away tears.

Dolly had a stubborn streak that would only make things worse for her there. The schools would not tolerate any child having a mind of their own. She was such a beautiful little girl and so independent. She seemed more like a little mother to Jacob and Rayen then a big sister. Always trying to help feed them and change Rayen's diaper. I missed them all so much. I shuddered to imagine her trying to fend for herself in those cold bleak buildings. The schools had changed a little but the foreboding atmosphere was the same. Aww and my little Jacob, he reminded me so much of my brother David. Such a tender and loving boy. He would never survive. Rayen with her big bright eyes. I smiled just remembering what a beautiful family I had. Sparkling eyes was my baby, Rayen. I would always call her sparkling eyes. She was so chubby and her eyes followed you wherever you went. I just wanted to hug them all, hold them close and tell them it would be ok.

When my kids came home I would take them to live by the Elizabeth Colony. The colony was close to Cold Lake. The reserve had a lot of lands there and it was isolated enough that no one would find us. I would raise the children there. I didn't need a man. I was more than capable of building a cabin for us to live in and living off the land. I prayed that until that day came that my children were living in a beautiful home with their father. Gary loved them and I knew he would take care of them.

It was only a few days later when my auntie came running into the house beaming from ear to ear. "Maria, Maria come quickly. A letter came for you. We opened it. The kids are coming home. Your kids are coming home."

I couldn't believe my ears. I fell to my knees and wept. It was a shock. An amazingly beautiful shock. The Creator had heard my prayers and he was bringing my girls and my boy back to me. I stood up and I couldn't help but do a little jig and then I grabbed my auntie and twirled her around. We both laughed and ended up in a pile on the floor and I started to cry again but these were tears of joy.

"Does father know? I asked. My heart sank as I realized the children would want to know where their brother Johnny was. More questions that were so hard to answer but I would deal with that when they got home. I would have to get them moved quickly. I knew the men would be back.

Oh my goodness, I had so much to do and no idea what to do first.

4 KATE

Jacob was wailing and I hadn't even hit him that hard. What a little whiner. Matilda came running in.

"Mommy, stop it, stop it." She wailed. "He's crying. Don't do that. Don't hurt him."

"Go upstairs," I said to Jacob. He turned and bolted for the stairs. Then I turned to Matilda. I leaned down and put my arms around her.

"Matilda, you're too little to understand. I have to smack Jacob. I have to smack him because he's really bad. He doesn't listen." I explained. "Mommy doesn't have to smack you or Sally because you're good girls."

Matilda looked up at me innocently and her only comment was, "Oh."

Sally came in at that time and stood quietly watching us.

"So you have to remember, don't bug Mommy when I do this O.K. because I have to do this for their own good." As an afterthought I said. "And don't tell Daddy either."

"O.K. Mommy, I won't." She said as she took off into the living room to play.

After Matilda had left Sally said, "Why are they here anyway, mom? Send them back. I know you don't want them. We don't want them either."

"Sally, you know I can't do that. Your father has decided that this is something that we have to do so we'll just have to make the best of it."

"I don't care what daddy says. Just send them back. I hate them." As she ran crying to her room.

I felt terrible. My girls were so good. My girls were so innocent and they had to live here with these other kids. I was sure it would have a detrimental effect on them. Well, I'd just have to make sure that it didn't. I would discipline these kids and I'd have to do it quick.

The phone rang and I hurried to answer it.

"Kate, hi it's Gary. I'll be coming over to see Jacob and Rayen today like we planned O.K.?"

"Sure Gary," I said. "Make sure you bring the money."

"I will." He replied. "I'll be there soon. I'm just at Linda's."

"See you soon," I said sweetly.

When I got off the phone I called Jacob downstairs.

"Go upstairs and be quiet," I ordered. "Don't make a noise or you'll regret it. And I mean it. Take your sister and make sure she doesn't cry."

I glared at him and then took the belt out of the drawer and just shook it at him. He knew I was serious. A few minutes later I heard Gary pull into the yard. I walked out on the steps wiping my hands on a dishtowel. As he walked towards the house I walked down the stairs to meet him.

"Hi, Kate." He said. "I'm here to see the kids."

I held out my hand and he passed me an envelope. I glanced at it and then slipped it into my pocket.

"Well Gary, I forgot you were coming to see them. Victor took them out and they're not here."

"What do you mean you forgot? I just spoke to you. Are they not here? You told me a few minutes ago that I could see them today. Why didn't you tell me that when we were talking on the phone?"

"Well, I figured you'd like to see me. I haven't seen you in a long time."

"Why are you doing this, Kate? They're my kids." He totally ignored my innuendo.

I heard a noise upstairs and I silently cursed Jacob. Gary looked up towards the bedroom window. I was hoping he wouldn't see his head pressed against the screen.

"Gary do we have to go over this every time you come here. They are not your kids. That was your choice, remember. Can I help it if their father wants to take them out and do things with them? Victor's more of a father to them than you'll ever be."

I could see the vein in Gary's head pulsating. He stood there for a few minutes and we just stared at each other.

"Fine Kate, have it your way. I just want what's best for them." He turned on his heel, walked back to his car and drove off. Well so much for an afternoon rendezvous. What a jerk! What he doesn't realize is that I have his children and I will do whatever in hell I want to do with them and there is not a damn thing he can do. "Come down here," I yelled.

I heard Jacob slowly making his way down the stairs. He was struggling to carry Rayen on his hip as he entered the room.

"Why can't we see dad?" Jacob asked as he placed Rayen on the floor.

"He is not your father. You will call him Uncle Gary from now on and I will decide when you see him. Do you understand? Don't ever talk to me that way. Now line up."

I walked over slowly and opened the drawer. As I pulled the belt out I said, "Who wants it first?

I would make Gary pay for what he was doing to me. I would make him pay dearly for treating me like dirt. It will be a cold day in hell when I'd let him see his little half-breeds.

And so that's the way things continued. He must have tried to visit every week for three months and then finally he took the hint and he just quit showing up. I heard he was working up in the mines. He didn't want me. I knew that now. I hated him.

The baby was really starting to irritate me. She had just turned two. She cried and hollered constantly. If it wasn't for a feeding then it was another shitty diaper. Normally when she really started to annoy me I would put her in the crib, close the bedroom door and leave her there, which is what I did today.

I heard Jacob tiptoe down the hall and enter the bedroom. At first, I was tempted to go after him and stop him but the baby calmed down when he entered so I left him. He was in there for about a half hour. In fact, I had totally forgotten about them. I heard the bedroom door open and I heard Jacob go back upstairs. Oh, the baby must have fallen asleep.

Good. I headed down to the basement to pick out something from the freezer for supper. I had no sooner reached the bottom step when I heard Rayen start crying AGAIN. I stomped up the stairs and headed right to go to the bedroom. I walked in and the baby was standing in the crib. I was thankful my mother had lent me the crib or there would be no way to contain her. I walked over to the crib and the baby raised her arms to me. I ignored her and reached in and smacked her on her soggy diaper. Damn it. Did she never stop?

She wailed louder from the impact and I hit her again. I kept hitting her hoping she would shut up. She didn't so I ran to the kitchen and grabbed the belt out of the drawer. I walked calmly back to the bedroom. Tears were streaming down her face. Well, if she thought she was getting any sympathy from me she was sadly mistaken. I pulled her out of the crib and holding her by the one arm I swung the belt and hit her with it. I had only hit her a few times and she stopped crying. Ah Ha! It worked I thought. I swung her around so I could see her face, and she had turned a deep purple color and she was gasping for air. I dropped the belt and shook her as hard as I could. Finally, she caught her breath. The little bitch. She did it to scare me. I smacked her twice more just for scaring me and put her back in the crib. She could cry all damn day for all I cared. I went back to the kitchen, turned the radio up and started to bake. Stupid child.

Just then I heard the school bus pulled up and as Sally got off the bus. My mom pulled up at the same time. Mom waited until Matilda got in the house and then just waved and took off. Oh, how I love my daughters. The little angels that they are.

And so the days progressed into months. Every day seemed to be more of a challenge for me. As the checks continued to come in Victor and I were able to get the rest of the house painted and insulated. I still had the agony of trying to discipline these two but they did what they were told now. They knew if they didn't there would be hell to pay.

Every Sunday we all showed up for church. Victor would help me get the children ready and we never missed a service. The weekends were harder for me to discipline the children but normally Victor was gone for at least a few hours each day, either helping his brother, or fencing or trapping so I was able to keep a steady regiment of strapping the children to keep them in line.

In the summer of '65', Victor convinced me that we should allow Dolly to come and stay with us. Just for the summer, he said. Reluctantly I agree. Dolly had just had open heart surgery and she had been in the hospital for just about a year. She was staying at the Combermere Convent now. I was just thankful they hadn't unloaded her here.

My sister Annette, and her husband, Davey were visiting from Peterborough. Her life had turned out exactly like she planned it. Davey and Annette had both finished high school, got married and moved to the city. Just the way I was supposed to. I loved to see her as much as the distance permitted but I couldn't help resenting her a little. They had two daughters.

Paula, nicknamed PJ, she's 5, and Karla. She's two.

Annette walked into the kitchen and said. "Kate, I have to go to Bancroft to pick up some pictures I had developed. I phoned this morning. They said they would be ready today. Do you mind watching PJ and Karla?"

"Sure Annette," I said. "No problem. You go ahead and take your time."

She hesitated. "Are you sure it won't be too much?"

"No, never mind," she said quickly as she changed her mind. "I will take PJ, Jacob, and Matilda. That way we can balance the load."

I laughed and gave her a hug. "Thanks, Annette. Always watching out for me, eh?"

"Well someone has to," she said as she rounded up her crew and took off to the car. It was only noon when they left but I decided to prepare supper. Stew will be fine. I thought. With a total of 11 people for supper tonight, it was an excellent choice. Dolly came in the door from feeding the dog.

"Dolly, watch Rayen and Karla while I make supper," I demanded.

Karla and Rayen were in the living room playing. They are both in diapers. I am in the process of potty-training Rayen. It wouldn't take too much longer. I didn't need any more shitty diapers to contend with.

"O.K," Dolly said and walked past me into the living room leafing through a comic book. I ripped it out of her hands.

"Do as you're told Dolly. You're just visiting and you have to pay your way."

I glanced into the living room periodically and I noticed Karla under the coffee table. I walked in and said.

"Don't go under the coffee table, girls." I glared at Rayen to enforce it and then smiled sweetly at Karla.

"Dolly, I told you to watch these kids." Dolly kept her head down and flinched as I went by. What a weird child. I returned to the kitchen.

A few minutes later I looked in again. Rayen was under the coffee table. Damn it. They never listen. That kid isn't too bright. I reached into the kitchen drawer and pulled out my strap. I keep it at the back of the drawer so Victor wouldn't see it. Well, I will show her. I marched into the living room. Rayen's shirt had slipped up and she was squirming around under the table giggling. I'll soon change that. I thought. I swung the belt. I made sure that it connected on bare flesh. A long red welt appeared immediately. I wasn't worried. I had specifically picked this belt because it didn't leave marks. I don't know how many times I struck her and then I realized Karla was crying. I picked Rayen up roughly and threw her on the couch.

"DON'T MOVE," I said. "If you move you'll get another one."

Then I directed my attention to Karla. I picked her up and said.

"It's O.K. honey, Auntie Kate is here."

47

I looked over at Dolly and said.

"What are you crying about? If you had been watching your sister none of this would have happened. You should get the belt too. You're lucky I have my hands full. Now go sit on the couch with your sister."

Back in the kitchen, I poured a big glass of milk from the fridge and then rummaged through the cupboard. Within a few minutes, I was triumphant and returned with a bag of cookies I had hidden in the back of the cupboard. I placed on the table in front of Karla and she gave me a big smile. She was happy again. I felt much better. I couldn't have my darling sister upset with me.

It made me extremely sad as Annette, Davey and their children piled into their van to return to Peterborough that evening.

It would be another week before we returned Dolly to the convent.

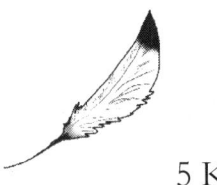

5 KATE

It started out as any normal day until the phone rang. "Hello," I said.

"Hello is this Mrs. Victor Gabbon?"

"Why yes it is, can I help you?" I could tell immediately that this was not just a normal phone call and I prayed that no one was listening in on the line.

"Brian Butler here with the Children's Aid Society. We have received a letter from Mrs. Martha O'Malley. She has some concerns regarding the children staying with you and we'll need to come by and see them."

"Of course," I said sweetly. "Just let me know when you plan to come."

"We'll get back to you and thank you."

"If it wasn't one thing it was another. I would be calling Mrs. O'Malley and giving her a piece of my mind. She should keep her damn nose out of my business if she knows what's good for her.

Rayen started saying "Napee, napee". I marched her into the bathroom and set her on the toilet. Jacob followed us and said. "She wants milk".

Little smarty-pants. He thinks he knows everything. A quick backhand took care of that. Jacob started to cry and after another few smacks both of them were crying. My god, this was getting hard on my nerves and my hands. I really needed to get a better belt to use on them.

I put Rayen in her crib and sent Jacob to his room.

It didn't seem to be very much later. I was lying on the couch in the living room and I looked up to see Jacob walk by me with a pencil. That little bastard better not be writing on the walls.

"Jacob, what are you doing?" I inquired.

"Nothing." He said and backed up.

"Don't be afraid Jacob. I won't give you the belt if you show me where the marks are."

Jacob smiled and ran over to the kitchen table. He crawled under and pointed up. I leaned down to look under the table. "Did you put marks anywhere else?" I asked him. He crawled out from under the table and headed down the hall to the bathroom. The bathroom was finally being installed. It was still under construction and Victor was planning to complete it when the girl's cheques came in this month. We had bought just about everything but we hadn't had enough money to buy the pipes for the plumbing and the taps.

When he entered the bathroom he took me to the far end of the bathroom and pointed between two of the studs. There were more marks there. I didn't say anything to him I just walked out to the kitchen and grabbed the belt. Jacob had followed me and I grabbed him.

"Don't you ever write on anything in here again." I turned him around and gave him three good smacks with the belt. Then I took him into the living room and set him on the couch. "DON'T MOVE," I screamed. "You can sit there until you rot. Don't move and don't you dare fall asleep."

Geez, my hand hurt. I really have to remember to use that belt. I rubbed my hand until it felt better.

This was getting harder and harder on me to try to keep these two in line. If Gary and I were together there would be none of this. I puttered around for the afternoon and periodically I would wander into the living room to see what Jacob was doing. The first time I went in he was just sitting there so I glared at him and left again.

The second time I went in to see him he had fallen asleep. I walked over until I was directly in front of him and yelled. "Wake up." I grabbed Jacob and shook him hard and then I walked away.

Just before Victor got home I told Jacob that he could go and play with Matilda.

At the supper table, Victor said. "Jacob, have you been crying?"

He kept his head down and in a quiet voice he said. "No."

Good boy. They were learning.

I piped up with, "He's got a bit of a cold. He'll just have to go to bed early. He'll be fine."

Victor seemed satisfied with that.

The following day I heard the phone ringing about 10:00. I picked it up on the third ring.

"Hello, Kate."

"Hi, mom. What's up?"

"Oh, nothing. I thought I'd come over and have coffee with you if you're not too busy."

"Sure mom. That would be great."

"O.K. then, I'll be over in about an hour."

We hung up and I got lunch ready for the kids.

After lunch, I put Rayen down for a nap. She must

have been tired because by the time mom showed up she was asleep. Mom showed up shortly after eleven and I made coffee for us.

Jacob and Matilda were playing in the living room. The children were having a disagreement about something or other. I walked in the living room.

"Jacob, it's time for your nap."

Jacob stood up and walked upstairs to his room. I went back to the kitchen and continued my conversation with mom.

"Kate, where is Jacob?"

"Oh, I sent him off for his afternoon nap. You know how kids are."

"Isn't Matilda going to have a nap too? They are about the same age, aren't they?"

I didn't want to argue with mom but I hated when she tried to tell me how to raise my kids.

"Mother, Matilda doesn't take an afternoon nap anymore. She is older than Jacob."

"Kate, somehow I don't think a month makes much of a difference at their age."

"I don't want to get into this with you, mother. You raised your kids the way you saw fit and I'll raise mine."

"Fine Kate, but people notice things around here. Annette mentioned it when she was visiting last time. I hate when you're the talk of the town."

"Don't worry mom. And Annette, she is so worried about being the perfect parent that she can't possibly understand what I have to go through. They're not angels you know. I do what I have to do."

"Well it's not my place to say anything but I think you should treat all the children equally."

"Mother, let's just drop it O.K."

"Fine, have it your way." She picked up her jacket. ""I heard Gary and Peter have been fighting about the kids. Gary says you and Victor won't let him see his girls."

"Mom, Gary hasn't bothered to even try and see them and if he wanted to, you know we would let him." These lies were starting to feel real now.

"Gary had to turn the kids over to Social Services so Dolly can have heart surgery. Poor little thing has a hole in her heart. I guess they are sending her to Toronto for surgery."

"So where is he staying now?"

"He got laid off at the mine and I'm not even sure where he is living now."

"He'll be fine Mom. You worry too much about... everything."

"Well, I better get going now. Matilda, come and give grandma a kiss."

Matilda came running in and threw her arms around her.

"Bye Grandma. Did you bring me some candy?"

Mom rummaged through her purse and pulled out a pack of gum. She handed two to Matilda.

"Give one to Jacob when he gets up, O.K. And you be good to your brother and sisters."

She gives her a soft pat on her bottom and Matilda runs off laughing.

"Thank-you Grandma."

"I'll see you later Kate, and think about what I said."

"Sure mom. I will."

Meanwhile, my mind was racing. What the hell was Gary up to? I would have to make sure we took him right out of the picture.

I looked out the window. I wanted to make sure that Jacob and Rayen were not picking on Matilda. They were playing on the swings. I watched for a few minutes. I noticed with satisfaction that Matilda got more turns on the swing than the other two. That was good. A funeral procession went by the house. I went out on the step and called Matilda. She came running into the house and I gave her some milk and cookies. When she was settled, I went back outside. I went over to the children at the swing.

"Jacob, did you see the big black cars go by?" I asked.

"Yes mom, I did." He said. He continued to push Rayen on the swing.

"You don't just keep swinging when a car goes by. Those are bad men sent by your mother to steal you away. If you see a car you run and hide. Do you understand?"

"Yes, Mom," Jacob said.

"Yes, Mom." Rayen echoed.

I grabbed the swing to stop it. "Jacob," I said. "Go and get me a branch from that tree."

Jacob walked over and tried to break a branch off. He was taking too damn long so I walked over and pushed him out of the way. I twisted off a branch a little longer than a foot.

"Get up I told him." He stood up and I dragged him over towards Rayen.

"Bend over," I demanded.

Jacob bent over and I smacked him as hard as I could with the branch. Whack! Whack! I looked at Rayen. Her face was already scrunched up and she was sobbing.

"Now you," I said to her. She wouldn't get off the swing. I grabbed her and pulled her off. She had her hands behind her back and she wouldn't move them. I tried to pull them away but she wouldn't budge. Finally, I got frustrated and said. "Fine," I said. "Jacob get over here. If Rayen won't take her spanking then you will take both."

He leaned over and I smacked him again.

She was crying loudly. "Shut up," I said. "Be quiet or he'll get it harder." Once I was finished with him I turned back to Rayen. "Do you want me to hit Jacob again?" I asked.

"No, no, no" she pleaded.

"Bend Over."

She bent over. She still had her hands covering her butt.

"Move them."

She slowly moved her hands to her sides and stood there trembling. I hit her a few times and then a couple more just because she pissed me off.

"If you ever try to stop me again you'll get it worse. Or your brother will." I said. "You never, never say No to me, ever, or you'll get it worse. Now march in the house both of you and go straight to bed."

Father Ginelli dropped by the house shortly after to tell me that Linda had sent a letter to Child Services asking that the children be returned to their mother. Geez, why couldn't everybody mind their own damn business?

"Kate, I know this will be hard on you but Indian Affairs has arranged for the children to be picked up in Belleville and returned to their reserve in Saskatchewan. A woman named Mrs. Theresa Okanee is coming from the Thunderchild Reserve to pick up all the kids and return them by train to Saskatchewan."

"OMG Father. We can't let this happen. Victor and I have become so attached to these children. They've been here so long. You have to do something?" My cash cow was going astray. I squeezed out a fake tear and wiped it away making sure Father Ginelli saw me.

"Oh don't you worry Kate. Tell Victor to meet me at the chapel tonight. I'll phone Peter to join us. We won't tell Linda or Mrs. O'Brien. They're causing problems but we'll figure something out."

I don't know exactly what happened at their meeting but Victor came home all smiles and told me we had nothing to worry about. The girls would be baptized on the weekend and given their new names. Jacob and Rayen would be staying. Whew! That was a close one. I would have to make sure no one in the godforsaken town knew anything that went on in this house. Those kids better not be running their mouths to anyone.

Victor took off the next day to take a trip to Belleville Indian Affairs Office with Father Ginelli and Peter. That weekend I had two new baptismal certificates in my hand with new names for Jacob and Rayen. God is good.

I went straight up to the girl's room and handed each of them a St. Christopher medal.

"Pin these on your underwear with these safety pins. Always wear them. Do not lose them. They will keep you safe."

I went downstairs and straight to my bedroom. I pulled a chest out from under the bed and neatly placed the new baptismal certificates in there for safe keeping. I would need those certificates to register the children in school. Children's Aid seemed to have backed off as well. Maybe things were looking up.

6 MARIA

The Elizabeth Colony was close enough to our reserve that we could still see my brother David, my father and the other family members. The children might be lonely at first but we would be together and in time we would be able to come back to the reserve.

I was so thankful I was by Gary's side every step of the way as we had built our cabin. Right from the tedious process of selecting each tree individually. He made me laugh when I would run to a tree and he would say, "Maria, that will never do." In his own handsomely rugged way he would direct me to the tree of his choice and somehow make it seem like it was the one I had chosen. We took turns chopping them down. One would chop while the other sharpened the axes. Then we would rest and eat dried meat and berries. Once the trees were down Gary would stack them on the dogsled and tie them down. He had shown me how to cut the notches into the logs so they would fit together perfectly. A mixture of moss and clay served as a bonding agent. My shoulders had ached from holding the heavy logs while Gary painstakingly placed each perfectly chiseled log into its appropriate position. We had made our home together. He was such a gifted man. He was fluent in Cree and he always reminded me so much of my brother David, right down to their mannerisms. It wasn't surprising that this was the man I had chosen to spend the rest of my life with.

I yearned for the many happy years we had spent together. Oh, to turn back time and have everything as it was. We did have such wonderful times and I missed him.

I immediately shrugged my shoulders as if to remove the bothersome thoughts. He was gone and I needed to make the long journey, to try and find us a place to live before the girls arrived on the train. I had more important things to do than reminisce about things that would never change.

It had not been hard for me to stay sober since I heard the exciting news of my children's return. I had a permanent smile pasted on my face and I filled my days picking berries. Saskatoon berries were my most favorite and they grew in abundance. The juice stained my hands and my lips and I would be thoroughly exhausted by the time I got home. In the evenings I took the time to work on my girl's clothing mending and altering to ensure they would have sufficient wardrobes when they came home. I could hardly wait to see their faces and kiss them all over. Had they grown much?

There is no greater loss to a mother, or father for that matter than to have their children ripped so viciously from their hands. No parent should ever have to feel this torment. My heart hurt for all the families that were not as fortunate as I. This was exactly what I was pondering as I drifted off to sleep that evening. I would not have to experience that pain anymore because my children were coming home. Except for Johnny. I shuddered and tried desperately to block the vivid images racing through my mind. I had a soothing mint tea and instead turned my thoughts to the homecoming. Father had already turned in for the night so I blew out the lantern and settled in for a wonderful sleep. I held my solitary picture in my hands as I prayed. The picture was beginning to fade. Gary was smiling at me with one arm around Dolly, who was our-years-old and his other arm on Jacob's shoulder. Jacob had just turned three. Behind them, you could see our log cabin and our car. I was pregnant with Rayen. I remembered fondly taking the picture. It was taken in Elkpoint, Alberta. I placed the picture down on my nightstand and tried to sleep.

I had no huge demands on my time the following day. It would be another few days before David would return from the Elizabeth Colony. David had offered to take the journey for me so I would be freed up to make all the other necessary arrangements.

I had barely closed my eyes and again I was caught up in the continuing saga which sporadically plagued my nights. This time, though, I was not alone in my fight. I felt little hands grabbing mine as I ran and as the light tightened its menacing hold on me I realized I had my baby in my arms. I couldn't see my other children but I knew that they were with me too and I awoke gasping for air and sobbing. Father was standing over me shaking me gently by the shoulder.

"It's just a dream, my girl. It's just a dream." He said as he pulled the covers up. "Go back to sleep." And he quietly left my room.

I was doomed. I felt an emptiness that I hadn't felt in months and I prayed that it was, just a bad dream this time. I tossed and turned but there would be no sleep for me now and as the rising sun flickered through the window dancing on my wall I debated whether I would even leave my bed that day. Maybe if I just stayed there the dream would erase itself.

I did fall asleep and awoke to darkness. I stumbled to the kitchen. I was familiar with the layout of the house but the blackness threw off my perception and I ran smack dab into a stand that father had made that stood in the hallway, stubbing my toe. Cursing quietly so as not to wake my father, I hopped to the kitchen. I had made bannock and it was still on the counter. It was my plan to grab some of the yummy Saskatoon jam I had made, with lard and salt but I dropped the knife which made a loud clatter on the floor. I stood very still listening for father but I heard nothing. Grabbing a piece of bannock for each hand, I hobbled back to bed.

I awoke the following day, prayed to the creator, finished smudging and exiting my bedroom I ran directly into father, nearly knocking him over.

"Oh, I am so sorry dad," I said.

As he gained his composure. "That's ok, you can't hurt me." He laughed. "Are you ok, my girl? I heard you get up in the night. You slept all day yesterday. I was concerned."

"I am more than ok dad. I've just been so excited about the kids coming home. They should be here within the month and I have so much to do to prepare. I'm sorry if I woke you. Would you like me to make some breakfast? It will only take a moment."

"I've already eaten my breakfast Maria but you should make more bannock." He said with a mischievous smile and I suspected he had finished off the last of it. "I'm off hunting. We are getting low in supplies. A couple of us are going to meet at the cabin by Turtle Lake. You know the one. There has been talk of a lot of deer in that area. I'll be back in a few days." And with that, he was off.

Well, that was good news. I loved the taste of fresh

venison and I could make at least one of my girls a new jacket, or perhaps moccasins for everyone, and hats as well.

Tomorrow I would make my way to the Band office and wait for the telegram to find out when exactly the children would be arriving from Ontario. I was so thankful that the train station was here. The only traveling would be to our new home. My brother David had graciously made the trip by himself and his description of the clearing he found for our cabin sounded nothing short of paradise. The trees surrounding the opening were as tall as the eye could see. The river ran close by with a breathtaking set of falls that would supply our water and had enough shallow areas that I would have no worries of the children playing or bathing. In David's exploring of the area he had found an abandoned cave that I could block off and use for storing food and meat. The land was thick with foliage, with berries growing as far as the eye could see. There were signs of numerous wildlife so I knew we would never go hungry. We were cutting it close in timing but the cabin would only take a few days to be ready for us. I had the privilege of watching our people erect ceremonial lodges within hours with precision so I had no doubts that everything would go as planned. We were indeed a skillful people and worked together as a community when anything needed to be done. I had already written Gary again to tell him the exciting news. Tomorrow I would find out exactly how many days we had to complete everything. With everything already packed. We were good to go.

I could not contain my happiness and that night there were no dreams.

Theresa Okanee dropped in shortly before lunch. She was many years older than me but her daughter, Tina and I were very close. I admired Theresa and was a little envious of the way she dressed and carried herself. I was so grateful to her. Theresa was an elder and had been designated by band council to take the long trip to collect my girls. I wanted to go with her but when I had approached Chief weeks ago to see if that was possible. His response was, "Maria, Indian Affairs has arranged for the children to be returned. It is their wishes that this is officiated by one of our elders. Theresa has graciously offered to take this journey and so that is what shall be done. We must follow the rules."

I nodded and walked away. Since returning to the reserve I didn't really feel that I belonged anymore. I did learn our language again and I tried to remember and relearn our culture and customs but I felt disconnected. There was something not quite right. I discussed this with father shortly after I had returned home but father didn't understand English very well and my Cree was so limited that communication was difficult. All he had said was, "It will take time my girl."

Theresa interrupted my train of thought when she said. "Maria, it is still early can we have a cup of tea?"

"Oh, what was I thinking, of course, Theresa. Come, come in, sit." I walked ahead of her into the living room and patted the seat on the couch. The kettle was still hot so I steeped some muskeg tea and returned to sit beside her on the couch. I must have had a peculiar look on my face because Theresa quietly said, "It will be ok, Maria. I will take good care of the girls. Don't worry." With this, I smiled not realizing I had been holding my breath and we finished our tea in silence.

It was a quick, quiet walk to the band office. I was thankful Theresa had come to keep me company. She understood my silence and I watched her lips move silently as if in prayer. Our elders were so knowledgeable. I looked forward to the days when I had that wisdom. I had so much to teach my girls. The band office was actually just a room in the rec hall. I sat down briefly on one of the two hard chairs but after a brief moment I stood up and wandered over to lean against the counter. Tick tock, tick tock echoed through the hall and I shifted nervously from one foot to the other as we waited for the telegram.

Theresa came up to me. Leaned in and whispered, "Maria, if you need to use the bathroom I promise I will be here." I smiled. "No, no, I'm ok, I'm just nervous." Soon we both heard the tap, tap, and tap. It seemed like hours before my cousin, Greta brought the single sheet of paper to the counter where we had stood for what felt like an eternity. I knew from her expression that I was not going to like what was written.

I tried to read it but I couldn't. Teresa gently took the paper from my shaking hands and then turned to me with tears in her eyes and said, "Maria, I am so sorry. It seems that Indian Affairs has reconsidered and feel now that it would be best if the children stay where they are." She touched my arm and I pulled abruptly away. "Maria, are you ok? Can I get you some water? You look terribly pale."

I struggled for words, "There has been a mistake. They told me they were coming home. They're coming." I started to wring my hands. I was not ready to register what was going on. "Maybe we can just go and take them. Chief has to be able to make them honor their agreement." I didn't realize but as I was talking my voice was getting louder and louder. There were only a handful of people in the band office and they were all staring at us but I didn't care.

"Oh, Maria. Try to calm down. We'll figure something out. Please don't cry." Up to that point, I didn't even realize that tears were streaming down my face, burning my eyes. All I could see was red. This had to be a mistake. The sinking feeling soon turned to anger and I began smashing everything I could get my hands on. Books, cups, papers flew in all directions. No, no, no, kept screaming inside my head. I felt arms grab me from behind. I fought with everything I had in me. The grip never loosened and my brother whispered quietly in my ear. "Maria, I'm here. Don't do this." With that, he gently turned me around, wrapped his coat around my shoulders as if to shelter me and marched me straight out of the building. I buried my head in his shoulder, sobbing as we walked down the road. We just walked and walked as I cried. David never said a word.

We stopped in front of a very familiar house. There was a rocking chair on the porch that I sunk into. As if reading my mind, David lit a cigarette and passed it to me. I don't smoke often but I needed one. I held it for a moment, the smoke spiraling through my fingers. I watched it mesmerized, numb to my surroundings. Finally, reality reared its ugly face and I inhaled deeply. It burnt my throat and I teared up again, starting to choke. I could hear people talking inside the house and then David reappeared very quickly carrying two bottles of moonshine.

Never had I wanted anything so badly. My children were my life. My family. How could I go on?

And then as angry and hurt as I was, it hit me. It didn't matter that Gary had taken our children. It was inevitable that no matter what we did, I would not be allowed to raise my children, any of my children. The government had stolen that right from me. None of our people had any rights. It didn't matter what kind of parent we were. It didn't matter the magnitude of families that they ripped apart at the core in the process. We didn't matter.

I had feared that the kids would be grabbed when they got off the train. Grabbed and taken to boarding school before I was able to whisk them away to our hidden paradise.

The thought of them not coming back had never even crossed my mind. No matter how I looked at it, it was hopeless. They were gone. Maybe for good, and there was not a damn thing I could do about it. My gut ached, my heart yearned and I had never felt so alone.

I should have known by the dream. But in actuality, I was living a worse nightmare right in this moment, worse than anything that could come to me in the night.

7 KATE

Today was a wonderful day and I was totally happy. Father Ginelli had called me today and asked me if we would like to take over the contract to clean the school. Mr. Winters was getting too old and had decided not to do it anymore. I was thrilled that he had asked me. I guess he knew how much it cost to raise four kids. I had agreed right away. The kids were still a little young but they'd still be able to help out. I waited impatiently for Victor to come home so I could tell him the good news. This would increase our income quite a bit and I could pack it away into our savings account. The school wasn't that big anyway. It consisted of two classrooms on the main floor. Grade 1 to 4 was in the one classroom and Grades 5 to 8 were in the other. Along with the two classrooms were two bathrooms, male and female and a small teacher's room with a small adjoining bathroom. The basement had an additional classroom that wasn't utilized that much which shouldn't increase the workload that much. The other part of the basement consisted of a recreation room, furnace room, and utility room. Father Ginelli had explained that we would only do the regular cleaning in the evenings and seasonal cleaning twice a year. He estimated that it would take between an hour, and possibly an hour and a half each evening.

I couldn't wait to start. He told me that I would get a monthly cheque for the job.

Rayen was the only one at home now during the day. One more year and she would be out of my hair as well. The other children were ten and younger but I knew we could do it. As I glanced at the calendar it amazed me that it had been nearly three years since Victor and I had made that dreaded trip to pick up Jacob and Rayen. I was thankful I had put my foot down right away to let them know who the boss was. It was paying off now and I laughed to myself. In more ways than one.

Today had been an exceptionally quiet day. I didn't find the need to discipline Rayen. It was a nice surprise. After the older girls left for school she entertained herself and managed to stay out of my way for the majority of the day. I noticed she was uncannily quiet unless she was being disciplined and she appeared to live in her own little world when the other children were gone.

She never acknowledged when I snuck up and spied on her. She would continue to babble on with her dolls like they were real people. It was when Jacob got home that they usually needed a beating for something. It seemed as soon as all the children were together my nerves got bad.

I had driven half way to Bentley's store today to get cigarettes before I realized I had forgotten her upstairs. The house was quiet when I returned and when I checked in on her she hadn't even noticed that I left.

"Get your coat" I yelled. Startled, she jumped. As I moved into the room she backed up like I was going to hit her. "Go, get in the car," I ordered.

She ran to the closet and grabbed her jacket. "Come on, come on, we don't have all day." She raced past me down the stairs and out the door. As I nestled into the car, she jumped into the back seat. I loved our new car. It smelled like a new car but it had put quite a strain on our budget but I smiled because now we would have more money coming in. Victor would be so happy.

After we left Bentleys we stopped at mom's house so I could tell her the good news but she wasn't home. I stopped to pick up our mail and as Mr. Montgomery handed me our mail he said. "Kate, do you know where Gary Gabbon is these days? That's your husband's brother, isn't it?"

"Oh, he is working up in the mines. And yes he is Victor's older brother. Why do you ask? I smiled.

"I have a few letters for him and we're not sure where to forward them."

"Mr. Montgomery, I can take them for him. He is always dropping by the house to visit his kids and I'll make sure he gets them."

"That would be so nice of you, Kate. I'll give you his mail from now on then. It's been here for a while and I thought I might have to return it." He passed me three letters and continued. "How are you and the family doing these days?"

"We are doing great." I was bursting to tell someone so I blurted out excitedly, "I got the contract to clean the school today."

"Good for you, Kate. You have a really good day." And with a wink, he was back to sorting mail. I slipped the letters into my purse with our mail and practically ran to the car.

A whole new world was awakening for me and I finally felt that everything would be ok. This boring mundane existence that I was currently moving through was starting to open up.

For those few brief moments, I was at peace. We even made one more stop at Bentley's store and got ice cream.

"Don't spill any in the car, Rayen." She was practically beaming.

Nothing would ruin this day for me.

The house as starting to really shape up, we had a new car and now a new job.

I was in such a good mood that I decided to make dinner. It was then that I remembered the letters. I ran for my purse and carefully pulled them out. Hmm postmarked from Saskatchewan.

I was starting to think that maybe Gary didn't want anything to do with me and as I read the letters I realized why.

My dearest Gary, I am still angry with you for taking our children but I know why you did it and I still love you. The government people have taken all the children including Johnny and I am so sad. Sometimes I just cry. Please tell me you are ready to send for me. I haven't touched a drop of alcohol. I have taken all the livestock including the dogs and sled to my father's place for safe keeping and I am staying with him now. All I want is for us to be together again as a family. I wait patiently every day to be in your arms. With All My Love Maria

I threw the letter on the floor and stomped on it. Stomped and cursed. That ugly bitch. That stupid ugly squaw. She was not coming here. I would not allow it. So that was his plan. I had half a mind to call him and I raced for the phone but as I pulled it out of its cradle I changed my mind and instead scurried back to rip open the second letter.

My dearest Gary, I have been informed by Indian Affairs that my auntie, Theresa Okanee will be coming by train to pick up the children and I am so relieved. I hope you are well. I have arranged to sneak away with the kids to our own little paradise in Alberta. I am hoping you will find it in your heart to come join us. Father and Johnny know exactly where we will be. I have quit drinking and I miss you terribly. With All My Love Maria

Well, I had taken care of that. There would be no precious paradise for anyone. I would make sure she never got her stinkin brats back. Their names were changed and there was not a damn thing Gary, Maria or anyone could do about it. Now I was in a foul mood. I needed a damn smoke. What was wrong with me? Why didn't Gary just stay with me like he was supposed to? He should never have gone out west. None of this should have happened. My dearest Gary my ass. I was so mad I spit on the floor and then yelled to Rayen.

"Get down here right now or I swear I will knock you into next week." She came running down the stairs looking bewildered. Bewildered and stupid as usual. "Get my cigarettes," I demanded. She ran to the counter and handed them to me. "Rayen, do you remember what I told you about why you and Jacob are here? She nodded her head no. "Well, of course, you don't remember. You're stupid. Now listen up and don't you forget it this time." I made my way outside and sat down on the step. She followed and sat down beside me. I stopped talking long enough to light my cigarette taking a long drag and exhaling slowly. "You and Jacob are here because nobody wants you. Your dad doesn't want you and your mom doesn't want you so we are stuck with you." Her eyebrows raised and I continued, "You and your sisters were so poor when you got here. You were covered with bugs from being so dirty. All your mother does is drink. She is a filthy squaw and you and your brother and Dolly are dirty little half-breeds. Do you understand? She nodded her head with big eyes.

71

"Don't ever forget that. If it wasn't for Victor and I, you girls would have nothing. Now say thank you, mom."

"Thank you, mom," she said.

"You can go to your room now. Just remember that is not your room and this is not your house." And she scampered into the house. The door slammed behind her as the school bus pulled to a stop on the road. The children were laughing and joking as they got off the school bus. I waved and smiled to the bus driver. Once he drove away I just sat on the step finishing my cigarette just watching them.

As soon as Jacob came up the stairs I said. "Go clean my bedroom and then clean Sally and Matilda's bedroom. I set out milk and cookies for my girls. Oh, they were such good kids.

"How was your day girls?"

Sally immediately started complaining. "Everyone is mean at school mom and I have a whole bunch of homework. It is so not fair. We shouldn't have to go to school. It is so boring."

"Finish up your cookies and milk and you can all go watch television until supper is ready."

"It was such a fun day mom we got to paint and Mrs. Thomas took us on a field trip….." Matilda was still talking a mile a minute as I wandered into the room where the children kept their school bags and rifled through to see if there were any notes from the teachers. Jacob was too stupid to give them to me so I had to look for myself.

I saw Jacob's math book on the cupboard and as I went through his school bag I found another one the same.

"JACOB" I yelled. Jacob stood before me within a few seconds.

"What mom?" he asked.

I held up the two math books. "Where did you get

these?" I asked gesturing towards them.

"Mrs. Thornton gave me that one." He said pointing to one of them. "Because I left mine at home."

"No, she didn't, did she?" That little bastard thought he was fooling me. "You're lying to me, aren't you? You stole it."

"No mom, I didn't. I'm not lying. She did let me borrow it. I will take it back tomorrow."

"You do not say No to me. You can take that book back tomorrow but you will tell your father when he gets home what you did. You will tell him that you stole it. Do you understand?"

"Yes mom," he said. He put his head down. His body was trembling so I knew he had started to cry. After supper, I said to Jacob.

"Isn't there something you were supposed to tell your dad?"

Jacob just looked at me for a second and then he walked over to Victor, who was still sitting at the supper table. He stood before him quivering and said,

"I stole this book from school."

I smiled satisfactorily. Then he said,

"But I really didn't." And he started to cry.

Victor jumped up off his chair. "Go to bed." He ordered the children. They all scrambled.

After they had retreated to their rooms he looked at me and said angrily.

"Kate, what the hell was that all about?"

"Nothing," I said innocently. "Jacob stole that book and I told him he had to tell you. I don't know why you're getting mad at me. I didn't do anything."

"You didn't do anything, eh. Well, then I really don't know what everyone is talking about."

"Talking about," I said a little worried. "What do you mean?"

"I mean you better lay off those kids. Other people

know what's going on here. We don't need any more shit. So cool it." With that, he walked out the door.

I sat there baffled. I wasn't doing anything. I don't know what his problem is but I'd let it go for tonight. I tiptoed up the stairs so Victor wouldn't hear me. When I got to the doorway of the room Jacob was in, I said.

"If you every cause any trouble in this house again I will kill you." I walked back downstairs.

As I descended the stairs I heard Sally say. "You heard mom Jacob. You better never do that again." She threatened.

I smiled. My daughters were so much like me. I retired to the bedroom for the rest of the evening. Crap my good news for Victor would have to wait. I heard him working away outside. It was a beautiful evening and I debated whether I should go out and join him but tomorrow was another day. So instead I climbed into bed and picked up the novel I hadn't quite finished reading yet.

The following day, Matilda, Jacob, and Rayen were playing outside. Sally had spent the night with my mother. It was a beautiful day. Finally some peace and quiet. I heard Matilda crying so I went storming outside to see what was going on. Matilda was sitting in the dirt crying her eyes out. I walked over to her.

"What is going on here? Matilda looked up and said.

"Mommy, Jacob drew a picture and he says it's me."

I picked up the crumbled picture she was referring to. It was a childish attempt at a picture of a monkey. I threw it back on the ground and grabbed Jacob by the cheek. I dragged him into the backyard with one hand and I hit him with the other hand. How dare he treat my daughter like this?

"You little good for nothing prick. You leave my daughter alone. You're nothing but a savage and a bastard. If you ever make Matilda cry again I will kill you. I swear to god I will, I hate you, you little prick."

I hit him a few more times and heard a car approaching so I took him in the house.

"Sit on that couch until your father gets home." Sally appeared out of nowhere and said.

"I'll watch him, mom."

A car pulled into the driveway and I went out smiling to greet my visitors. It was Father Ginelli and Martha O'Malley. I wonder what they want. I hope they don't want to come in and visit. I was relieved when Father Ginelli stayed in the car and Martha approached me.

"Father wanted me to let you know that Dolly made it through the heart surgery yesterday with no problems. I know that we were all praying for her and our prayer was answered. Father Ginelli wanted me to tell you himself but it's been such a long trip and his leg is bothering him. Dolly is still really weak but the doctors say that she is making excellent progress. She'll be in the hospital for about a year. I knew that you would want to take the children to see her. She would enjoy the company." With a big smile, she continued, "Her dad was at the hospital today when we left. He brought her a dozen red roses. They were just beautiful. I gave her the card you sent too."

"Oh, you must both be exhausted. Could I offer a cup of coffee?"

"No, no, we just wanted to stop in quickly." Glancing towards Father Ginelli she said. "Well, I better get going now and get Father home. He is so tired. He didn't sleep at all while she was under. He was so worried."

"You thank Father Ginelli for me and thank you for dropping by," I said sweetly.

She retreated to her car and they drove off. I still hated her for calling Children's Aid but I hadn't heard anything from them at all. I shook my head after they left. Yah, like I'm going to waste my time dragging these kids across the country to visit poor little Dolly. The only way I would be taking them to a hospital would be to commit them. This made me chuckle. Thank God! That was one brat that I wouldn't have to think about for a while.

8 MARIA

After the initial shock of finding out my kids were not coming home, it became a vicious cycle for me of binge drinking, sobering up, crying and occasional fits of rage. This horror was much greater than residential school or even death. I had been able to survive residential school and any deaths on the reserve, we all gathered as a community and there was a comfort knowing that the person had returned to the spirit world. They were at peace.

The not knowing where my girls were, how Jacob was, or how they were doing, ate away at me constantly, ripping my insides apart like the constant heartbeat with a slight murmur. Where every once in a while, just for a split second there is a pause but then it resumes. Giving me brief moments where I could remembering the good times before the steady beat of hopelessness and emptiness resumed. My memories were beginning to fade. Not much but the little faces were not as clear as they once were. I clung desperately to them amidst spontaneous tears. It was alcohol that numbed my pain. Enabling the illusion that in fact, everything was ok for a bit and as I sobered up it all came flooding back. Therefore after waking up continuously at the house of the man who made moonshine it seemed only practical to move in. These days stretched to months.

Walking by the long mirror in our bedroom one day I was startled with the reflection staring back at me. Instead of the strong, beautiful woman who kept herself so neat that I was so used to seeing, I was aghast to see a thin, unkempt waft of a woman. I would be lucky if I had the strength to hold a rifle. A shell of the woman I had once been. My children had been gone nearly a year.

It was in that moment I decided to go to Edmonton. It was Edmonton Child Services that had taken the girls so many months before. It was them that decided to give the temporary custody papers to Gary's mother. Temporary did not mean forever. I marveled in the simplicity of it all. I was going after my kids. I cursed myself for not thinking of it earlier.

Without so much as a goodbye, I raced to my father's house. The house was in darkness and though it saddened me to leave but I felt strongly that this was my destiny. I threw a couple pieces of clothing into a bag and grabbed my picture of my family. I kissed it for luck. Next, I went to see my brother, David. His wife had left him the previous day and I felt so bad for him. I considered asking him to join me but I knew he was in no frame of mind to travel so I didn't bother. A quick hug from him and I was off to the train station with its memories so cold and ugly.

Edmonton was a three-day walk. I knew this because of my nephew, Jeff, crazy bastard that he was got stranded there one summer. He was such a nut that he didn't even bother to wait for a ride. He just walked home. He slept for most of a week by the time he finally got home and he limped badly but he made it. He loved to tell this story when we were drinking. I know he embellished quite a bit because the one time he told it he stopped to snare a rabbit and the next time he actually chased it and caught it with his bare hands. I'm not sure to this day if there ever was a rabbit. What a guy!

I could hear the train long before it arrived. Climbing on I looked longingly back at the reserve. I would return and I would have my children. I flopped down on a seat, placing my bag on the seat beside me. The car I was in was totally empty. That was good because I didn't feel like making small talk with a stranger. I leaned back, slipping my shoes off. It would be a long trip. I felt bad for not saying goodbye to the man that made the moonshine. I knew his name all along, Jeremy, but giving him a name somehow meant giving him a small piece of my heart and I wasn't prepared to relinquish anything. I ran my finger across my eyes still feeling his lips where he had tried so hard to kiss my tears away. I outlined my plush full lips and then pulled my hand away, feeling guilty. Somehow I felt betrayal to Gary whom I would soon be rejoining. Within minutes I was asleep.

I was so thankful when I finally got off the train and stretched my legs. It had been a long trip. Well, here I was. Edmonton air even smelled better as I refreshed in the slightly brisk breeze. The leaves were starting to turn color.

I would need to get everything done quickly in order to reach Ontario before winter. I wandered around just enjoying the scenery and I walked by the park. I spotted a couple native guys sitting on a bench talking so I wandered over and sat not too far from them under a tree. They glanced over periodically and finally the cute one approached me. "Well hello, beautiful lady." Was

his opening line. I laughed and smiled. "Hi, I'm Maria."
My name is Mike, and my friend's name is Mike but just
remember I am the cute Mike ok." He winked and
reached down offering his arm to pull me up. I reached
back and dusted off my butt before going over to meet
the other Mike. Neither of them was hard on the eyes
but I did have to admit cute Mike was cuter. It wasn't
long before we all wandered down to the local pub. It
was so busy here in Edmonton. Nothing like the reserve
back home. I went into the bathroom to wash up. It was
dull and a little gloomy but there was running water. As
I splashed water on my face I started to feel better about
the trip. Tomorrow I would go to Child Services and
find out the address for Gary's mother. They had
approved the temporary order for my children to go to in
Ontario. It was time for them to come home. The cool
water was refreshing. I felt hunger pains ad pulled some
dry meat out of my bag. Once I had the address it was
just a matter of making my way to Ontario. I really had
no idea what to expect when I got there but they are my
children and I would figure something out. I returned to
our table with the two Mikes. I hadn't been gone that
long but there already six beer sitting there and two
placed sat directly in front of my chair. I hadn't really
planned on having a drink but a couple wouldn't hurt.

The jukebox was blasting out a song that for some
reason made me extremely sad. "It is the evening of the
day..ah.ah.ah.. I sit and watch the children play.
ah..ah.ah. Smiling faces I can see, but not for me,"
blared out of them speakers I swiped a cigarette out of
the pack on the table and ran to the door, knocking over
my beer but I didn't care. The cool air hit me in the face
and I sat down on the step wiping tears away. A few
seconds later cute Mike sat down beside me and gave me
a light.

"Are you ok, Maria?"

"I'm fine, just fine. That song just reminded me of my kids."

"Oh were they taken?" he asked.

"No, no, I am getting the address where they are tomorrow and I'm taking the train to Ontario to pick them up." I smiled. "We have a perfect little getaway where we are going to go."

"How many kids?"

"Four, 3 in Ontario and my boy, well he was taken to residential school here. Two boys, two girls." I sighed. "My kid's father took three of them to his mom."

"There is no way you are old enough to have four children, Maria. Well good for you. I know everything will turn out fine. I'm so glad I met you, Maria. Now come, we'll have a glass to celebrate."

One glass turned into so many that I lost count. I was having so much fun. We had only been there for a number of hours when the door to the tavern swung open and a very voluminous woman walked in. She scanned the room briefly and walked straight to our table.

"Mike, get your ass home right now. You better not of spent all the money neither." She was leaned right into Mike, then she swung around and directed her attention to cute Mike, "And you, my sweet brother, go home." I told your wife if I sawn you in here I would send you home to take care of your baby." And with that, she stormed off.

Cute Mike grabbed my shoulder as he walked by and winked. "See you Maria, best of luck." And they were both gone.

Once they left, the bar actually started to creep me out so I finished my drink. I was thankful they had left the smokes on the table so I gathered my belongings. I asked the bartender for a pack of matches on the way out. Now where to spend the night.

It was starting to get cold. I should have worn a

warmer jacket. I had to find Oxbridge Place. I needed to get Gary's mother's address. Oxbridge Place was where Gary and I had gone when they took the kids the last time. I remembered what the building looked like. It was huge. Gary and I had spent more than half an hour trying to find our way through it to find out where to go. I wish he was here to help me. I had to get used to being by myself.

I had no idea where I would spend the night. The beer had made me tired and as I turned a corner, I caught a figure and it looked like he was following me. I sped up, pulled my light coat tighter around me and walked faster, just shy of a jog. I kept glancing back and when I thought I lost him, I slipped into an alley and sat down by a dumpster to collect my thoughts. Within seconds the glare from the streetlight was blocked by a dark shadow. I scrambled to my feet and raced down the alley but there was nowhere to go.

"Come on, sweet thing," I heard him yell. "I got something for you." He grabbed me from behind groping at my breasts. His breath stunk of alcohol. I threw my arms back and pushed my butt out throwing him off balance.

As he grabbed at me again, I turned swiftly. All my survival instincts kicked into high gear and the hunter in me emerged. I lunged at him, head butting him in the throat. As he gasped for air I grabbed him by the hair with both hands yanked his head down on top of my knee over and over. I pushed him and kicked him square in the groin. As he leaned over I kicked with all the strength I could muster and caught him directly in the stomach. He went flying back, arms flailing and I heard a thud as he hit the ground. I pounced on him. Out of the corner of my arm, I saw his arm coming as if in slow motion and I heard a distinct crack. The pain seared through my nose and eyes. I was dazed, but only briefly.

Sitting on him I threw punch after punch after punch. I could feel blood spraying on my face. It was warm but I didn't stop. It seemed like hours before I was pulled off. I'm sure it was only minutes.

It was only when the policeman had me cuffed and I was sitting in the car that I started to breathe again and thought, "Oh My God, what have I done?" The policeman asked me my name and what happened and I did my best to explain. "He attacked me," I told him. I spotted my picture lying on the ground. "Can you please, please get me my picture?" I begged. "It's right there on the ground" I pointed. "Please, it's all I have left." He ignored me. It must have fallen out in the struggle.

I watched as two men in white picked up that piece of crap and put him a stretcher. Don't step on my picture I prayed. Don't, don't, don't. They were coming closer and closer and then the wheel of the stretcher rolled right over it. The only real memory I had left and it was gone. We started driving away.

"Why are you taking me?" I asked. "I did nothing wrong."

"Yah sure you didn't" I don't think that's what that poor guy on the stretcher is going to be saying." At that point, I just quit talking. I knew where I would be spending the night.

It was three weeks before I appeared in front of a judge, and another three before I was sentenced. 7 years I got. 7 years for defending myself. His lawyer had made him out to be this amazing family man, with a good job and that I tried to rob him that night and then beat him. He was white and as much as I tried to tell anyone what had really happened, I was ignored. Well, at least he didn't rape me. I had been through that enough.

In another twist of irony, it was me being escorted to another government facility. Institutionalized once again for something that was not my fault.

9 KATE

The year was 1969. Rayen had started school this year, Matilda and Jacob were now in Grade 4 and Sally was in Grade 7.

I was working away in the kitchen when I heard Sally call Rayen. Rayen came scrambling from the basement and ran upstairs where Sally was. After a few minutes, I saw Rayen go back upstairs. "You stupid idiot." I heard Sally yelling. "I told you to get my book. Can't you do anything right." I ran to the bottom of the stairs. "I didn't remember what you asked me to get. I'm not stupid." I traveled up the stairs quickly and grabbed Rayen by the shoulder.

"Are you talking back?" I asked. Rayen didn't answer. "I told you never to talk back now come downstairs right now." I marched her downstairs and set her at the kitchen table. She started to cry. "Go downstairs and get me an onion." Rayen stood up and returned with the onion. "Sit down," I said. She obliged. I stood at the counter and slowly cut the onion into small pieces. I pulled the frying pan out from the drawer in the stove and put a little bacon grease in it. "Stop crying," I ordered again. Rayen's sobs subsided to sniffles. Rayen hated onions. I cooked the onion and placed it on a plate. Then I turned and placed it in front of her at the table. "Eat it all or you'll get it." Rayen picked up the fork and put a tiny piece in her mouth. She gagged and spit it back out. "You will sit at this table until you eat it. All of it. Do you understand?" She nodded. I stood there and watched as she ate piece by piece. She was swallowing them whole. "Chew them." She continued to cry. She was still sitting there a couple of hours later when Victor returned home from work. He walked into the kitchen and sat down. "What is she doing?" he asked. "She has been very bad today and I know you don't like when I punish them so I am making her eat onions as her punishment." Victor glared at me and said.

"Rayen, go to bed." She got up from the table and ran upstairs.

"Victor, I don't know what you expect. Do you think I should just let these kids run the house? When their bad I punish them. You're the one that brought them here. Just remember that."

Victor looked at me tiredly, shook his head and went back out. I heard him drive away. He returned a few hours later and didn't mention it again.

The next day we took a trip to the Madonna House in Combermere. I bought most of the kid's clothes there. It was a second-hand store and it had a wide variety of items. Sometimes I bought clothes for my children there as well. Sally usually complained though unless the clothes were brand new. I was rummaging through a bin when I found two winter hats. One was furry white and it had a black strip down the middle. It looked like a skunk. I laughed and placed it with my purchases. The second hat was green and had little projections on it.

This one could pass for a porcupine. I decided to buy it as well. After I had made my purchases we drove home. The next morning when the children were getting ready for school I gave Jacob the green hat and Rayen the white and black one. That would teach Rayen for fighting with Sally yesterday. She had to learn that she was the gopher and to me that meant gopher this and gopher that and don't talk back. The other kids should have a great time with these. Sure enough, I received a phone call from the principal a few days later.

"Hello, Mrs. Gabbon."

"Yes," I replied.

"I just pulled Rayen off of Bob Brown. They were having a terrible fight. I'm not sure exactly what it was about but I think it had something to do with a hat. Both of them will receive the strap today. I just wanted to phone you and let you know. I will be phoning Bob's parents as well."

"That damn kid. She is always doing something. O.K. I know that you're always having problems with Rayen so you just do what you have to do. And be sure that I will thoroughly punish her when she gets home."

"I think the strap will be sufficient. I've spoken to both children and they now understand how wrong it is to fight and they've promised that it won't happen again.

"Well it sounds like you have it under control so I'll leave it up to you then. Thanks so much for calling."

When the children arrived home I noticed that Rayen didn't have a hat on.

"Where's your hat?" I asked her.

"I don't know I think I lost it."

"Where is it?"

"I'm not sure maybe I forgot it at school."

"If you tell me what you did with it, you won't be punished."

"I threw it in the garbage." She said quietly. "All the

kids were teasing me."

"You threw it in the garbage. Do you think Victor and I are made of money? Do you know how much we have to go without because we have you stinkin brats? If we didn't have you kids we'd be rich. We could buy whatever we wanted. But no, we have to feed you and clothes you and take care of you. Victor and I work our asses off to support you and this is the respect we get. And fighting. You embarrass us by picking a fight at school. I think it's time that you girls got a haircut. That's what I think. Get in the kitchen. Matilda did Jacob take off his hat today."

"Yes, mom he did."

"Jacob, that means you too. I'm cutting your hair."

"Mom I have to go to the bathroom first."

"Fine go ahead."

Jacob emerged from the bathroom a few minutes later. I got the scissors from the drawer.

"Sit down," I told him.

He sat down and I proceeded to start cutting chunks of hair from his head. The dark hair fell in clumps onto the floor. After I had chopped off a sufficient amount I turned to survey the damage.

"There. Now thank your sister because you can both sit on the couch until your father gets home. Move it."

Next, I turned and motioned Rayen for her turn. The comb caught in her curly hair and I yanked it through angrily. As I snipped away I watched the curls fall tumbling to the floor.

She had been crying so much that little pieces of hair stuck to the tears on her face. After I had removed most of her hair I called Jacob out from the couch to sweep up the hair.

"Rayen get in the bathroom and wash your face. You look like a pig."

After she returned from the bathroom she stood in the

kitchen.

"Well, what are you waiting for? Get in on the couch. Don't move and no sleeping. Jacob, I will be in there in a minute. And there better be no talking either or you'll get it."

When Jacob finished he went to sit on the couch I heard him say. "Thanks a lot, Rayen.

Like the hat wasn't bad enough. At least I could take it off."

"I said no talking," I yelled in.

They were both quiet. A few minutes before Victor returned home I told them to go to their room and do their homework.

As I walked past the mirror in the bathroom I noticed I was starting to get wrinkles. These children were making me old. I didn't know how much longer I could put up with them.

As the seasons continued to change, so did my wrinkles and I wasn't the least bit happy about it. It was a struggle for me to get through each day. Everyone and everything irritated me. The only really consistent thing was strapping those kids and going to Sunday mass. I had given them their medals and they consistently lost them. It didn't matter how much I hit them they never seemed to learn. How could they be so stupid? It was my intention to never hit the children on Sunday but it was inevitable that one or more of the three would annoy me to a state that they needed to be lined up. The convent had closed so Dolly was now living with us as well. I received a larger cheque for her in lieu of her heart surgery so I had taken it in stride. I had more money to spoil my children.

Each morning all the children would pile onto the school bus and I finally had some peace and quiet. I filled my days reading paperback novels or listening in on the party line. There were 3 lines attached to our phone so when it rang for one of the other parties I would pick the receiver up very slowly, cover the mic and listen in. I was able to keep abreast of all the juicy gossip. I always hoped to hear someone mention Gary. It made me happy for a few minutes anytime I heard his name but then I would get very angry to the point I thought I might just explode.

After school, there were numerous chores to be completed. This usually involved me giving them the strap for one reason or another. Supper was a time where we all sat down as a family. I allowed no water on the table. It was my belief that it would cause you to choke on your food. My daughters were allowed to drink milk and of course, Victor could have whatever he wanted. After all, he was the breadwinner and head of the household. I let him believe this, though I knew it wasn't true.

There was a daily mass each morning before school that I hoped would cleanse the demons from these children but it didn't seem to work. After supper, Sally and Matilda could go do their homework but normally they ran for the television to fight over which of the 2 channels they would watch. The other children would do the dishes and then I piled Dolly, Jacob, Rayen and usually Matilda into the car to go clean the school. It normally took us about an hour and a half if the children didn't dally and if they did what they were told. In the winter months, it was completely dark by the time we got home. Sometimes I allowed them to watch television once they finished their homework.

Saturdays were the big day for cleaning so I got them out of bed bright and early. There was always something to keep them busy whether it be weeding in the garden, trimming the lawn, additional cleaning required at the school, laundry, mending or whatever I deemed appropriate. No one could ever imagine the magnitude of things that I needed to contend with. This house didn't run itself.

I was day dreaming and it was a wonderful dream. Gary and I were walking on the beach at Lake St. Peter. He had just told me that he loved me and I could hear ringing. I was sure it was wedding bells and I looked up at Gary patiently waiting. I knew he was going to ask me to marry him. I could still hear ringing. Finally, I jumped out of bed and ran to the kitchen. I don't know how long it had been ringing, but I grabbed it.

"Hello"

"Hello, is this Mrs. Victor Gabbon."

"Yes, it is" I replied.

"This is Mr. Webster from the Children's Aid Society. I was wondering if it would be convenient to drop by and see——" I could hear him ruffling through papers. "Yes, it would be Dolly, Jacob, and Rayen today."

My heart felt heavy. "Right now" and I panicked momentarily. "Yes, yes you can but what do you want?"

"Standard procedure ma'am. We've received a letter concerning the children's welfare and need to come by and ask a few questions. Would that be all right?"

"Of course," I said. My mind was racing. Who the hell was messing with my life? "Of course, you can. The children are at school right now but you could drop by at 4:00 if that's O.K."

"That's fine, Mrs. Gabbon and I appreciate your cooperation. I'll see you then." With that, he hung up. I was totally irritated. Getting woken up from a wonderful dream just to find out that someone was trying to cause trouble. I immediately called Gary.

He answered on the second ring. "Hello"

"Hello, Gary," I said.

"What do you want?" he asked dryly.

"Did you call Children's Aid? Are you trying to make

ROSIE CHRISTIE

trouble? Cause if you are I'm packing up these kids and throwing them out on their ear. Do you understand me? Don't screw with me Gary because you know I mean it."

"No Kate." he implored. "I have no idea what you're talking about it." Then with a note of concern, "Why is there a reason for concern?"

"Of course not, Gary." I spat out. "I just figured you were trying to cause trouble for Victor and I."

"No. I wouldn't do that. I just want what's best for my kids."

"How many times have I told you, Gary? They are not your kids anymore." With that, I hung up.

Jerk. He really pissed me off. When I have a coffee I'll make sure this house is spic and span. Don't want those Welfare people to think I'm a pig. I looked at my watch. 12:00. I had lots of time.

By the time the children got home the house looked immaculate. I didn't like having to do this work myself. That's why I had those brats. I was pissed off by the time I was finished but I greeted them warmly at the door.

"Hi, kids," I said. They all gave me suspicious looks. I went towards Jacob to give him a hug and he backed up.

"Ow, Mom. He stepped on my foot." my youngest daughter whined hopping around on the other one.

"That's O.K. Matilda. He didn't mean to."

Matilda gave me a bewildered look. I smiled sweetly and said.

"Go on upstairs, girls. There are clean clothes laid out on the bed. Make sure you put them on and don't get dirty. Matilda, you don't have to. Just grab some cookies and go downstairs and watch TV."

Matilda threw her school books on the kitchen chair. A few fell to the floor, and she went begrudgingly downstairs. I followed her downstairs and said.

"Matilda, a worker is coming to see how the kids are. You stay down here and be good O.K."

"How come a worker doesn't come and see me?" she asked.

"Because you are loved, honey. You are our daughter so it's different. No one will ever give you away." was my response. Then I hurried back upstairs.

Jacob was the first one to come downstairs. When he hit the bottom stairs I was there. I grabbed him by the arm and pulled him to the side.

"Listen Jacob. A man is coming to see you guys today. Don't you dare say anything about what goes on here or I will kill you! You know that, don't you?"

I leaned towards him threateningly. He pulled back from me and backed up against the wall.

"If he asks you any questions you say you're happy. Don't think I won't hurt Rayen and Dolly too, if you say anything. You don't want that do you? Now go downstairs and watch television with Matilda until I call you."

He retreated swiftly downstairs.

Rayen was the next one to venture down. She's only six so I wasn't too worried about her.

When she walked in the kitchen I said.

"A man is coming to see you. He wants to know how happy you are here. You are happy here, aren't you?

"Yes," she smiled. She was always trying so hard to get my approval.

"Scoot downstairs then," I said and smiled sweetly.

Dolly wasn't downstairs yet. What was taking her? I went up after her. She was sitting on the bed. She hadn't even started changing.

"What the hell are you doing?" I yelled at her. "I told you to get changed. You wouldn't want anything to happen to your brother or sister because of your stubbornness. Would you?" Then I changed tactics.

"You're a happy child, Dolly. When Mr. Webster comes today you tell him you're happy and you don't want to leave." I walked over and shook her. "You tell him that."

I went downstairs quickly to make coffee and put out cookies for our guest. They hadn't bothered coming for years and now just because Dolly was here. Now they had to come and check. It infuriated me but I kept my cool.

I called the children downstairs to sit on the couch and wait.

We waited until 4:30 and finally the phone rang. "Mrs. Gabbon, This is Mr. Webster. I seem to be lost. I won't be able to make it out to visit the children. I am so sorry for the inconvenience."

"Oh don't you worry. That's fine. It's been no bother at all." I said sweetly.

As soon as I hung up I turned and went back to the living room. The kids were still sitting on the couch.

"See it's just like I always tell you. Nobody wants you. That man called and said I am treating you so well that he doesn't even have to come here." I said. "Nobody cares about you and they never will. Now go and set the table for supper. And have any of you did your chores? I doubt it. Change out of your good clothes and move it. I want them done before Victor gets home. "

They immediately scurried upstairs.

I turned up the radio and then snuck up the staircase. I got about three steps from the top and I stood there listening. Jacob and Dolly were talking as they changed.

"Why didn't he come?" Dolly said. "If someone comes I'm gonna tell them what she does to us."

"No Dolly, please," Jacob whispered. "She'll kill us. I don't like it here either but there's nothing we can do."

At that time I ventured up the rest of the way and stormed in the door.

"So you don't like it here, eh? You don't know anything. I tell you over and over. No one wants you. What are you going to do? Where will you go? A couple of filthy half-breeds. You're lucky Victor and I took you in."

I looked them up and down in disgust. "When you came here from out west you were poverty stricken. You were like those children from third world countries. You were filthy and dressed in rags. Your bellies were all swollen up and you had Impetigo. Do you know what that is? That's what you get from being dirty. Edna had to burn your clothes and tie you to chairs so you wouldn't scratch from all the body lice. And you think you'd rather be somewhere else. Like anyone would take you. Don't you think if anyone wanted you, you'd be there? Victor and I took you in out of the goodness of our hearts. You little bastards are very, very lucky. Now I told you to do your chores so quit dawdling." I ordered. "You all, make me sick."

The next day it was about eleven when I heard the knock on the door. I ran to answer it thinking it might be Gary. I had been thinking about him a lot lately. When I opened the door it was my cousin, Geoff Woods.

"What a surprise Geoff. What are you doing around this area? My god it's been at least ten years since I saw you last."

"Hi Kate, I got a call from Mr. Webster. He wanted me to come and check on some children in this area. I'm working with the Children's Aid in Bancroft. I had no idea it was you I was coming to see." As he gave me a big smile. "So did you and Victor adopt some children?"

"Oh god no," I said shaking my head. "Victor's brother's kids are staying us for a little while."

"Oh, oh I see. They must be a school eh?"

"Yes, they get home about 3 o'clock." I was really hoping he wouldn't come back at 3. I was a little concerned that Dolly might say something.

"Kate, there is no need for me to see them. I know you and Victor and it would just be a waste of everyone's time." He reached out and shook my hand and pulled me in for a quick hug.

"I'll fill out my reports when I get back to the office and if you need anything you just call me Kate," and with that, he climbed back into his car.

I stood on the step and lit a cigarette and watched him drive out of the driveway. Well, that was a close fuckin call. I hope this was not going to become a habit. I felt a headache coming on. These children were nothing but trouble. I was thankful it was my cousin that showed up and not that Mr. Webster.

10 MARIA

It had been an uphill battle since I was released from prison. I was escorted to Onion Lake reserve where I was born. I visited various family members camping on their couch for a few months.

I had only completed 5 years and three months of my sentence and then been let out for good behavior. All while I was serving my time I had mentally prepared to travel to Ontario but as the years went by I began to lose hope.

I was thankful to be back with family. I continued to write letters and try to get different agencies to try and help me find my children but each time I thought I might have a lead I would get a letter back saying my children could not be found. They had disappeared.

After a few years of drinking, I woke up in on the Kehewin First Nation reserve in Alberta. It had been a night of partying.

The house I woke up in was nice. I didn't remember coming here. I was on a brown plush velvet couch and was covered with a warm quilted blanket. I pulled off the blanket and folded it and made my way to the kitchen. I checked the fridge and there was more than a dozen beer. I just heard the hiss as I popped the lid when I heard someone come into the house. I peeked around the corner to see my cousin Edward. I set my beer down and ran to give him a hug. I hadn't seen him in years.

"Oh my god, Maria. Where have you been? You look like hell." He said laughing. "Come, my wife is about your size. You can pick some clothes from her closet and have a shower."

I laughed and followed him as he grabbed some towels out of a closet and pointed to the bathroom door.

"Edward you look great. How the hell did I end up here?"

Edward looked at me shaking his head with a big smile. "You showed up with Daniel and Freda in Uncle John's old truck. I can't believe you guys made it. You were pretty tanked and I put you to bed on the couch but that was after you sang us a few songs at the fire."

I held my head wishing the pounding would stop.

"You can shower in there. He pointed down the hallway again with his lips. The lock sticks on the bathroom door but just shake it once you're done and it will open.

Next, we entered a bedroom. Just a mattress on the floor but it was made up and the curtains were pretty.

Edward watched me as I looked around. "I did ok eh Maria. I have been working as the garbage man here for about three years now and my wife, Caroline works at the children's home. Take anything you need and if you don't find what you need there, check the dresser too. There are a couple of us out back cooking on the fire. Come out when you're ready."

I could smell wild meat cooking and realized I was starving. It didn't take long for me to find something to wear and get showered.

As I walked out the back door I heard people laughing.

"Maria, grab some beer and come join us." My cousin yelled.

I was struggling to carry six bottles of beer to the fire and one of the men jumped up and came to help me. His long hair was braided and reached the middle of his back. He was quite handsome.

"Let me help you." He said smiling taking four bottles from me. "I'm Matt by the way. Where has Edward been hiding you?"

"Oh, I just got here. I'm from Thunderchild."

"Of course you are. I should have known. That's where all the beautiful Cree woman come from."

I blushed and we hit it off right away. Matt was so easy to talk to and we had lots of things in common. I liked Matt instantly. He was kind. I could see it in his eyes.

We became inseparable. Matt was caring and he drank with me. I was able to tell Matt everything. Eventually, it got to the point that he would hold me when I cried. Matt didn't have any children of his own. He welcomed me into his home. It was a beautiful house with 5 bedrooms. It needed a woman's touch and we enjoyed decorating it. It really felt like home. We had many friends and if we didn't have money to drink there was always someone that did.

Matt would drive me to Bonnyville to mail letters to the Children's Aid in Ontario. He would take drinking as I hit a dead-end, after another dead-end but I refused to give up.

One day I was walking home from the store. Matt had gone hunting in Frog Lake. Normally I would go with him but I was depressed and just wanted to stay home. He would be home tonight and I wanted to make him bannock so I walked over to the store for flour. I was a little hungover and stopped under a tree to rest and drink some water. I had just finished my water when I heard someone call me and I turned towards the sound. The church door was propped open and a nun came out the door. She came towards me and I looked behind me, but there was no one there. She sat down beside me. This made me very uncomfortable and I started to get up.

"My name is Sister Pauline and I can see by the look on your face that you have probably been to residential school and you do not like me."

I didn't answer so she continued, "I just want you to know that I am here if you ever want to talk. I do know some of what you might have been through, and it was wrong. What happened to you and so many others was wrong, terribly wrong.

I started to cry and as I walked away she yelled, "Come anytime and we can just sit together if you like."

When I got home I put the flour on the table and I cried. I just cried and cried. By the time Matt got home I was feeling much better and the smell of fried bannock filled the house. Matt had brought home a young buck so we spent the night skinning, cutting and packing. In the wee hours of the morning we were finished and sore and happy, we crawled into bed knowing we had enough food to last us for months.

The next few days I thought about Sister Pauline but it wasn't until a few weeks later that I ventured back towards the church.

Sister Pauline spotted me right away and came out to sit with me. She brought us each out a muskeg tea and we sat and sipped it. I didn't talk to her and she didn't try to talk to me.

It was on my 4th visit with her that I told her my name and we started to talk. Soon I found I looked forward to seeing her and I started going a few times a week, and then every day.

We talked about lots of different things. I finally felt comfortable enough to talk to her about some of the painful things I had been through and I asked her if she could help me find my children. She said she would try to help me. I finally felt like things might change.

Sister Pauline seemed to understand why I drank and asked me if Matt and I would like to come to AA classes.

I started attending the AA Meetings and after a few months, Matt and I were both attending AA and staying sober for longer periods of time.

After our two-year sobriety celebration, Sister Pauline asked if Matt and I would like to attend the Alcohol and Drug Addition Counselling Course being offered. It was an 8-week course and we agreed. The 8 weeks flew by and we both passed. I made me feel good to learn ways to counsel and help our people. I was starting to feel a lot better about myself.

It was after we had received our certificates that Sister Pauline came to our house. "Maria, I have sent a letter to the Children's Aid in Ontario again for you. I was speaking to someone at Indian Affairs and that particular Children's Aid Society has been requesting information about your Rayen and her status."

I couldn't believe my ears.

"Can I send something too? Will you help me? I want them to know that I want custody of all my children."

"Of course Maria. Come to the church tomorrow and we will send it off ok. I am so proud of you, Maria and I am so happy for you. You are a good woman."

I told Matt as soon as he returned home and as usual, he just smiled and hugged me. A little later he came into the bedroom while I was getting ready for bed. He put his arm around me and said, "If we are going to be a family don't you think we should get married?" Then with a twinkle, he stood up and attempted to pull something out of his pocket. I heard a clink, clink, clink, as a gold band fell and rolled across the floor. We both dropped to our hands and knees trying to find it. As Matt pulled it out from under the dresser I held out my hand and he slipped it right on. My heart felt good. This was the man I wanted to spend the rest of my life with.

As we laid in bed that night I was happy that I had found Matt but my heart ached for my children. Some day we would be a family. I knew Matt would be a wonderful father.

I was just drifting off the sleep and Matt whispered, "My Auntie Norma is coming to visit tomorrow."

The next morning I awoke bright and early. I made a wonderful moose stew and fried bannock. I had been up since 6am preparing, unsure of what time she would arrive from Edmonton. The house was spotless. Matt went outside to cut the grass and work in the yard. Matt had told me so much about his auntie Norma. He had lived with her when he left residential school. His mother and father had been killed in a car accident. He didn't tell me too much about it and I knew that was very painful time for him.

I heard a car pull in and I waited inside so Matt and his auntie could have some time together before she met me. I thought I heard the door open but no one came in so I leaned far out the window trying to see what was going on.

I felt someone grab my butt cheeks and squeeze quickly. I whipped around and I was face to face with who I could only assume was Matt's Auntie Norma. First, we were both shocked and then we both started to laugh. As Matt walked into the kitchen from the hallway

I realized that Matt and I were both wearing white shirts and black pants. With our long dark hair, Auntie Norma had mistaken me for Matt.

"So I see you've met Auntie Norma," Matt said chuckling. "And what have you two girls been up to?"

We had a wonderful day together and I had never met anyone quite as entertaining as Auntie Norma. She told me story after story about Matt and I could understand why Matt spoke so lovingly about her. She was a wonderful woman. I was sad when she said she had to get back on the road. I packed her a sandwich and we made plans to go visit her in Edmonton.

I would never forget how we met and even years later I would see her and she would cup her hands and squeeze and we would both start laughing.

It was about a month later as I was visiting Sister Pauline that she asked me to sit down with her.

"Maria, I know it has been extremely hard for you without your children."

Even now the pain when I thought of them brought tears to my eyes. I nodded yes, and she continued.

"You would be a wonderful mother, Maria. You have so much love, and you and Matt are really working hard. Do you think you two might ever consider taking in some children? Foster children? There are so many children that need a warm loving home."

"I, I, I'm not sure." I finally blurted out. "I need to go home now."

I walked very slowly on the way home pondering what Sister Pauline had said. In my heart, I felt I would be betraying my children somehow. I should have my children. I should be a mother to my children.

Matt knew something was wrong the minute I walked in the door.

"Maria, what's wrong my love?"

I explained what Sister Pauline had suggested and I

explained how I felt.

"Matt what would my children think?"

"Maria I think your children will love you regardless. Have you heard anything about them? Has anyone written back?"

"The last letter Sister Pauline received was regarding Rayen and they say they don't know her. That was the agency asking about her status. How can they not know her?" the frustration I felt was so overwhelming I thought I may be sick.

Matt took my hand, "Maria I know this is hard on you but maybe we could take in a child or two. Help some other children that don't have anywhere to go."

"Maybe," I said.

It took me a little over a week to decide and then Matt and I both went to Sister Pauline.

"We would like to help if there are any children that need homes."

"Oh Maria, Matt that is wonderful to hear. I am so happy that you have made this choice. When you're ready we can go to the meetings. I will go with you."

And so within the month we had our first little girl. She was 3 years old and her name was Mandy. Mandy was the first of many that would make their way through our door over the years. Matt and I loved each and every one of them.

It brought me great joy to be able to give so many children a home where they were loved and I enjoyed all the time I spent with each and every one of them. In the back of my mind, I wanted my children. These should be my children. It was not fair.

11 KATE

Saturday morning I called the girls about 7:00 to clean the school. Dolly, Matilda, Jacob, Rayen and I piled into the car. As soon as we entered the school I told Dolly and Jacob to go and fill the metal pails to scrub the floors. I send Matilda around to empty the garbage cans and put Rayen to work cleaning off the boards, spraying them and wiping them down. Next, I ventured downstairs to see what the girls were doing. When I entered the utility room Jacob had the pail draped over the tap as it filled. I walked in and smacked him in the back of the head.

"How many times do I have to tell you to hold that damn pail? You're going to break the pipe and I'll end up paying for it."

He immediately lifted the pail off and held it. His arms shook under the pressure. Dolly was waiting to fill her pail. As soon as Jacob's pail was full I handed it to Dolly.

"Carry that upstairs," I ordered.

About halfway up the stairs Dolly set it down and stopped.

"What the hell are you waiting for Christmas?"

"I'm sorry mom, I'm kind of tired and I just need to rest for a second."

"Tired. Why the hell would you be tired? You don't do anything around here anyway. You're a lazy little bitch. When I tell you to do something I expect it to be done now. Not next week. Now move it." She was always trying to use that stupid heart surgery excuse on me. Well, that had been years ago.

She carried the pail up the remaining stairs. When she got to the top of the stairs she said.

"Where do you want me to put it, mom?"

"Put it in Mr. Keller's classroom."

I watched her struggle to carry it into the classroom. When she returned I said.

"No, put it in the other classroom."

She glared at me but she obeyed.

"Now go down and tell your brother to hurry up. I don't want to be here all day."

Jacob appeared at the top of the stairs before I finished speaking.

"You and Jacob go and wash the bathrooms. Do a good job. I'll be checking and it better be clean."

After they went off to do that I walked into the utility room upstairs and grabbed a broom. I walked into the classroom and started to sweep. It didn't take me too long and it was complete.

"Jacob, go and get me a mop," I instructed.

When he appeared he had the mop. I grabbed it from him and mopped the floor.

"Dolly, go and dump this water and get me some fresh stuff." Dolly came in.

"Can I dump it outside?"

"No, carry it to the basement and make it snappy."

Rayen entered.

"Are you finished cleaning all the blackboards?"

"Yes, I finished mom."

"Fine, go and help Matilda empty the garbage cans and then take them downstairs and wash them out."

Matilda walked in eating a bag of chips.

"Where did you get those?" I asked.

"In the teacher's room. There's a whole bunch so they won't miss one."

"How many times have I told you that you just can't help yourself to whatever you want?"

"Sorry mom," she said and continued munching. She sat down at the teacher's desk and put her feet up. She sure was putting on weight. I'd really have to have to talk to her about that.

"Well stay out of my way so we can finish up." Dolly finally showed up with the clean water.

"If you and Jacob are done the bathrooms then you sweep the other classroom. Jacob can mop behind you."

Within a half hour, we were finished. I walked around and checked all the work.

"Who cleaned the girl's washroom?"

"I did," Jacob said.

"Well go in and clean the mirrors again. They're streaked."

I swung out my arm as he walked by and smacked him hard across the ass and my hand stung.

"Don't ever make me have to tell you to do something twice."

"I'm sorry mom."

Dolly said. "Do you want me to help him?"

"No, he can do it himself."

We stood at the front door waiting for him to finish. Once he was finished I didn't even bother to check it. I knew he wouldn't screw up twice. We drove home in silence.

When we got in the house I said.

"I'm going back to bed. Clean up around here and do your chores. Dolly peel a pot of potatoes for supper. Oh, and your Uncle Gary is getting married tomorrow. Get your dresses ready. Jacob, there is a pair of Victor's pants and a shirt you can wear. Gary has never, ever had the time to be with your kids. Never loved any of you but he's getting married." With that, I stomped back to my room. I was in a foul mood. Gary was getting married tomorrow. Linda had phoned to give me the lovely news last week. There was no way in hell I was taking them but they didn't need to know that.

Mom called and wanted all the girls to come and spend the night with her. I took Sally and Matilda after supper and dropped them off.

"Where are the other girls?" she inquired. "Oh, Gary came and picked them up," I said. "Oh how nice for them," she said as she bustled my girls into the kitchen. I could smell cinnamon. She must have been baking all day. The girls would love it. Once I got home it was quiet and I was thankful to relax and have a quiet night.

The day started as any other. I got up early and made Victor breakfast. It was Sunday. Today was the day. Victor was off to help Peter put up fencing at the farm before the wedding. The cows had gotten out twice this week. Where had this stupid week gone? I was tired and miserable but I stayed up and poured another coffee. I cried for a few minutes and then I wondered if Jacob finished the ironing like I told him to do yesterday. With the thought still fresh in my mind, I went down to the basement to see. The clothes were on hangers and there were a few items still bundled up in the laundry basket. I kicked it across the room.

Those kids couldn't do anything right. I grabbed a few items off of the hangers and threw them on the floor as well. I marched upstairs, caught my breath on the main floor and then proceeded up the last flight to the bedrooms. Dolly and Rayen were lying sleeping in the bed on the right and Jacob was sprawled out in the other one.

I yelled, "GET UP."

I strode to the side of the bed. Jacob was on the outside and I grabbed him by the ear and pulled him out of bed. He wasn't quite awake so I shook him.

"Did you do the ironing I told you to do yesterday?"

"Yes," he mumbled.

"Well you didn't do a very good job, did you?"

I felt my blood pressure rising. Why did these kids never do what I wanted? I turned to look at Dolly. She was awake now and had pulled her legs around so that her feet were on the floor.

"You. Go down and do the ironing. Pull all that crap off the hangers that Jacob thought he did yesterday and do it again. Do you hear me? Move it."

Dolly made a bee-line for the stairs. I still had Jacob by the ear and I let go.

"You, make these beds. It looks like a pigsty in here and then go downstairs, and clean mine.

Make it snappy."

Rayen piped up. "What can I do? I want to help."

"Help your brother up here," I said. "When you're done you can have some breakfast."

I went back downstairs, straight through the living room and into the kitchen. Where the hell were my smokes? I spotted them on the cupboard by the canisters. Was someone trying to hide them? I thought. I pulled one out of the package and lit it. Then I reached in the cupboard for an ashtray and made my way to the couch. God, I was tired. It was so hard watching all these damn kids. Victor had it so easy. I scrubbed and cleaned and cooked. I damn near broke my back but did I ever get any recognition. NO!

I could hear the kids upstairs arguing about how to make the bed. I was going to yell for them to be quiet but then I thought, fuck it. It's not worth the energy. I dozed on the couch for a while. When I woke up Jacob and Rayen were in the kitchen. Jacob was pouring cereal into two bowls on the table.

I strode into the kitchen. He hadn't heard me and I knew I startled him.

"Don't make a mess," I said, "and clean up these dishes when you're done."

At least they had gotten dressed. Then I made my way quietly down the stairs. I bet I'd catch that little bitch sleeping. As I came down the basement stairs into the rec-room I admired the new paneling on the walls. When the cheques came in next month, Victor and I would install a bar at the end. I deserved it with all the crap I had to put up with, with these brats. I walked into the room adjoining the rec. room. It has a cement floor. The wringer washer, ironing board, and freezer is in here. Dolly was struggling to adjust one of Victor's shirts on the ironing board. Well, she was working. Lazy bitch I was shocked. I didn't bother with her and returned back upstairs.

I walked down the hall to my bedroom. The bed had been made. It wasn't a perfect job but I didn't care. I sprawled across it and picked up the romance novel I was reading. I couldn't remember the name of it. It didn't matter. I knew the ending of this story. It was just like all the others. She would find her perfect man and live happily ever after. Yah, like that, ever happened. It sure as hell hadn't happened to me.

The kids must have snuck back upstairs. Well, good riddance. I was just relaxing and getting into my book and I realized I needed a cigarette.

"Rayen" I hollered at the top of my lungs. "Come

here."

I heard a patter down the stairs and Rayen came running in.

"What mom?"

"Go, get my cigarettes in the kitchen."

Off she ran. I heard her go into the kitchen and then I didn't hear anything for a few minutes. What the hell was she doing? Then I remembered I had left them in the living room. She'd find them. It took her awhile and she finally returned with my cigarettes.

"What took you so long?" I grumbled. "And did you bring the matches."

"No." was the timid reply.

"Well stupid. How am I supposed to have a smoke without a light? You're not too bright are you?"

She gave me a bewildered look and disappeared. She was back again within a few seconds and handed me the matches.

"Now, get out of here," I said.

I heard her scamper back upstairs. Around lunchtime, I wandered downstairs again to see if Dolly was done. Christ, it took her forever. She did do a better job than Jacob, though. I walked in took a quick look through the clothes. I couldn't find anything too wrinkled so I told Dolly to come upstairs to have lunch. When they all sat down at the table I proceeded to make lunch. I threw a few cups of water into a pot and made Kraft Dinner. The kids scarfed down their food down and cleaned up the dishes.

"Should we get ready for the wedding?" Dolly asked.

"Do whatever the hell you want. It's not like he wants you there anyway. He hasn't even tried once to come see you or help out with money. He's a loser and you are all going to turn out just like him."

I sat at the table when they left. I ate a little bit but I wasn't too hungry. I made myself a coffee and sat down at the table. I wasn't feeling very well. I looked out the window and lit another smoke. Rayen came into the kitchen, reached into the cupboard for a glass and proceeded to pour herself some water from the tap. Just as she went to take a drink she dropped it. The glass smashed on the floor. I jumped from the chair and grabbed her. I shook her as hard as I could.

"You stupid, stupid idiot. How can you be so clumsy?"

"I'm sorry. I'm sorry." she was saying.

I had her by the shoulder and I reached in the drawer for my belt. It wasn't there. Those little bitches had hidden my belt. Well, I'd show them. I grabbed for the rolling pin but it wasn't there either. I pushed her and she went flying. I'd find something, I thought. They wouldn't get away with this. I'll beat the living shit out of her and when I'm done the other two will get it.   I started pulling everything out of the kitchen drawers. I finally gave up.

When I turned around Rayen was lying on the floor. There was a puddle of blood by her head. That little fake I thought. I went over and leaned down to shake her again. She was limp. I grabbed her wrist and couldn't feel a pulse. Oh God, what have I done? My god I've killed her. I jumped up quickly and looked around. I picked her up and ran out the door.

Should I call a doctor? No, the nearest hospital was miles away and what would I say. I set Rayen down in the grass and ran into the shed. I grabbed a shovel. I ran out into the backyard wondering frantically what I could do.   I ran past the old outhouse into the bush.

About twenty feet back I started digging a hole. I dug faster and faster. My arms and back ached. Oh God, what am I going to do? The hole was getting bigger. It felt like I had dug for hours. When the hole was about four feet deep I slowed down. I dug for about another foot and stopped. Then I walked back to the house and picked up Rayen. I carried her out to the hole and threw her in. Now for the other two, I thought. I went back to the house and a voice I couldn't quite recognize as my own called out.

"Dolly, Jacob come here for a minute."

The two children appeared at the top of the stairs.

"Come here," I said. "Something has happened to Rayen."

They came running down the stairs and followed me outside.

"Back here," I said.

I crossed the yard and started into the bushes. I looked back every few minutes to make sure they were still with me. As I approached the area I had dug the hole at, I said.

"Hurry, Rayen fell down that hole."

Dolly was in the lead and leaned over to take a look.

"Go down there and see if she's O.K," I said.

Dolly glanced at me and then concern towards her sister overwhelmed her and she cautiously jumped in. I looked at Jacob. He had a scared look on her face and he was backing up slowly. I reached down and grabbed the shovel. By the time I had looked up he had cleared the bushes and was running across the yard. I chased him. When I was close enough I swung the shovel. It caught him in the back of the head. Blood flew. I felt it as it hit my face. It was warm and sticky. I wiped it off with the back of my hand. I could taste the blood.

Jacob fell on the grass. I reached down and swept him up in my arms. One arm encased his legs, to protect myself from him kicking, and I raced back to the hole. As I got closer I could hear Dolly yelling and crying. I leaned over the hole and dropped Jacob in. He landed with a thud. Right on top of Dolly. Dolly fell too under the pressure. I picked up the shovel and started filling in the hole as fast as I could.

"Stop it, stop it." I heard Dolly screaming hysterically.

She was crying and looking at me pleading to pull them out. I worked frantically shoveling dirt into the hole. My pulse was beating so hard I could feel it in my chest.

Then I felt a tug on my arm. I looked down and Rayen was beside me. I was sitting at the kitchen table.

"Mom, can I have some water please." I heard her say.

"NO," I screamed as I jumped up. "GET AWAY FROM ME."

I jumped up from the table and raced down the hall to my room. My heart pounding erratically. I was disoriented. How long had I been out? Minutes? Hours?

Victor arrived home shortly after.

"Kate, are you and kids ready?" he yelled from the door.

"I'm in the bedroom."

He appeared at the door, "You're not ready." He said. I could hear the disappointment in his voice.

I gave a little fake cough, "I've been throwing up all morning."

"Well should I take the kids to the wedding by myself?" he inquired.

"No, no, I really don't want to be alone. I'm too sick."

With a sigh, he walked back down the hall and I heard the door slam.

I began to cry and clutched my heart. How could he do this to me? How could he marry that whore? He would never see his children again. I would make sure of that. If I had to kill them myself.

12 KATE

Sally had been out late the night before. She was seventeen now and wasn't home very much these days. I wasn't sure what time she had gotten in. I heard a creak on the ceiling. I looked up. Someone was up. Jesus, I don't know how many times I told them to stay in bed until I said they could get up. I knew it was Rayen. How many times did I have to tell these children? I had told her over and over, but she never listens. As I ascended the stairs I heard her jump back into bed.

I walked into the bedroom. I saw Rayen's head on her pillow. She had her eyes pressed as tight together as she could get them. She couldn't fool me. I walked in and pulled the covers back. I pulled her by the hair until she was upright and then I smacked her in the head.

"How many times do I have to tell you to keep your ass in bed until I tell you that you can get up? I'm the boss. You know I'll smack you when you do this. Why don't you ever listen? Christ I'm going to smack you into next week. I am so sick of your bullshit." Rayen whimpered. By that time Jacob, Dolly and Matilda were awake as well. Great.

"Fine, now that the whole fuck'n house is awake, you three can go out and weed the garden. Move it." I leaned over and tousled Matilda's hair and said. "You can come with me."

I heard Jacob as I went down the stairs.

"Thanks a lot, Rayen. Why don't you just stay in bed? You always get us in shit." he said as they got out of bed and got dressed.

I scowled at Dolly as she walked out the door. The three of them could stay out there all day. Meanwhile, I had another pressing issue eating away at me. I had been keeping a close eye on Victor and Dolly. I saw the way he looked at her. She was flaunting herself for him. Fifteen and already a slut. Well, that was no surprise. She thinks I'm stupid. When she came down to the bathroom she would let her housecoat come undone. She thinks I don't see what she's doing. Well, I'd really have to start keeping my eyes on her. How could she do this, he was her uncle. I would have to keep a close eye. Maybe I could talk to Rayen and get her to spy on them for me as well.

That evening the girls were all downstairs watching television in the rec. room and I heard Victor call Dolly to help him. I waited a few minutes and then I snuck down the stairs. I walked swiftly to the door to the other part of the basement. The door was slightly ajar and I slide over tight against the wall so that I could peek through.

"Dolly, help me lift these furs down."

Victor had started trapping during the winters for extra income. He had a number of stretched and dried furs of muskrat. The furs were hanging from a beam in the ceiling. I watched as

Victor reached up to unhook the fur from the holder.

Dolly was facing him and reached up to help him lift them down. Their hands reached the top and I saw Victor lean forward. Did he press himself against her? I drew back quietly and returned quickly back upstairs.

So there was something going on. I was outraged. I paced back and forth in the living room wondering what I should do. I should just go upstairs and throw all her clothes out the window. That little slut was trying to get my husband. A few minutes later I saw Dolly come swiftly around the corner. She had tears in her eyes and she ran upstairs to the bedroom. Ha, serves her right, throwing herself at him like that. He must have said no.

I'll just have to keep a better eye on her. I won't let them be alone. I'll talk to Sally tomorrow and ask her to keep an eye on her too. That little home wrecker wouldn't screw up my marriage. I wouldn't let her. On second thought, I think those kids are due for another haircut. I smiled as I envisioned what she would look like when I was done with her.

Victor would have no interest in her when I was done.

I awoke with a smile on my face. The Indian Affairs cheque should be coming in for Dolly today. Great I could go out and buy Sally those new jeans she was bugging me about. Maybe I'd buy Matilda something too.

Mid-morning I walked to the end of the driveway to check the mail. I felt inside the mailbox but there was no mail. I was a little surprised. Maybe the mailman was late. As I walked into the house, a stack of mail on the counter caught the corner of my eye. I walked over and shuffled through them looking for the cheque. It wasn't there.

Where the hell was it? Who had brought the mail in? I went storming into the bedroom. Rayen was on the bed reading a book.

"Did you go and pick up the mail today?" I asked.

"Yes." she said with her head down.

"Did you give Dolly anything?" I inquired.

"Yes mom, a letter," She replied. "It was addressed to her." She continued defensively.

My money. She was giving that filthy tramp my hard earned money. I smacked her across the face and yelled, "If you ever do anything that stupid again I will kill you. You bring me the mail from now on. I don't give a shit whose name is on it."

The blood drained from her face and she hung her head.

"Rayen, go and feed the animals," I yelled.

A few minutes later I heard Rayen putting on her coat and boots. I walked to the kitchen sink so that I could get a good view out of the window and waited patiently for the show. All the girls were afraid of that dog. I don't know why? I had snuck outside earlier in the day to loosen the dog's collar. I thought it might be fun to untie it. He really was a good dog. When I went out to see him today he had wagged his tail and waited for me to pet him. I ruffled his hair and played with him for a while but it had rained earlier and I didn't like the dog smell. I had immediately gone into the house to wash that wretched smell off of my hands.

The kids always freaked out. They were always making a fuss about something or other. We hadn't even named the dog. It had been diagnosed as mentally retarded by the local vet but it was one of our best hunting dogs. Hunting season would be here soon. Victor loved that dog.

I saw Rayen return from feeding the pigs. I had thought the dog would chase her as soon as she went out in the yard but it looked like he was sleeping. She made her way cautiously over towards the dog house. She was about 10 feet away from the dog house when she pulled a huge bone out of the pail and threw it into the dog dish. I don't know how many times I had told them to place his food in his dish. The dog lunged. Normally the dog would run at the girls until it reached the end of its six-foot chain and then it would flip in the air and land on its back. Today, I watched as it kept coming. Rayen realized at the last second that the dog wasn't stopping and she turned and ran full throttle back to the house. She still had the tin pail in her hand. She was no match for the dog. It outweighed her by at least fifty pounds. Within seconds it had launched onto her forearm. I watched as it ripped through her coat. The blood gushed out like a fountain. I chuckled to myself and then looked around to see if anyone else was in the kitchen. Nobody, good. This was pretty comical. As I looked back out through the window Rayen started hitting the dog over the head repeatedly with the pail. He finally let go and she came screaming into the house.

I met her at the door and said.

"What the hells the matter with you, screaming like that." She held up her arm to show me.

"The dog" she sputtered out.

I leaned closer to get a better look. There was a six or seven-inch gash down her arm.

"Calm down," I said. It's not like your dying or anything. Come on, I'll bandage you up and don't bleed on the floor."

I made my way to the bathroom. Rayen followed silently behind me. I pulled some white tape and gauze out of the medicine cabinet. I turned around and she hadn't even removed her jacket. She looked quite pale. What a wimp.

"Well take your damn coat off so I can see your arm."

She removed her coat slowly. I peered closely at the wound. It was quite impressive. It wasn't terribly deep but it was long. Jacob walked into the bathroom. He looked a little pale as he surveyed the damage.

"What happened?"

"Rayen wasn't paying attention as usual and the dog got her."

What was all the hubbub about? Rayen would enjoy the attention from being wounded.

"Get out of the way," I said as I pushed Jacob to the side. He had moved closer to Rayen to get a better look.

"Keep your arm still."

I started wrapping the gauze around it.

I kept wrapping and wrapping but the pink kept peeking through. Shit, now I'd have to buy more. Finally, as I finished off the roll and taped her up I looked over at Jacob. He was still standing there watching.

"What are you looking at?" I said.

"Nothing. Are you going to take her to the doctor?"

"No, she'll be fine," I said. "Now take her upstairs and make her lay down for a while."

Jacob reached around to support Rayen as they left the bathroom. After they departed I thought. God, I had expected some excitement but not quite that. I should have sent Jacob instead. It would have been more of a fair fight.

Vem was in a foul mood when he returned from work so I didn't mention the incident.

I sent Jacob upstairs with Rayen's supper so that she wouldn't have to come down and told Victor that she wasn't feeling well. Once Victor had retired to the basement I called the kids to go and clean the school. Jacob was just finishing up the dishes. Sally came into the kitchen.

"Mom I have a huge English exam tomorrow so I'm going to stay home and study. O.K."

"Sure honey, you go ahead."

Rayen came slowly into the room supporting her

injured arm.

"Get in the car," I ordered.

"Hurry up," I said impatiently to the other two. "We don't have all damn day."

I went to the basement stairs and yelled.

"Matilda, Come on, we have to clean the school."

She came begrudgingly up the stairs and said.

"How come Sally doesn't have to help?"

"Now Matilda, you know she is in high school and has to study."

"So are the rest of us. Except for Rayen, of course. Get her to help you."

"Don't sass me, Matilda. Now go and get in the car."

I glared at Jacob. Just to let them know that I wouldn't put up with them speaking to me like that. I would really have to talk to Matilda. She knew better than to act like that, especially in front of them.

When we got back from cleaning the school it was about 7:30.

"Do your homework and get to bed," I ordered.

As I heard them traipse upstairs I went down to see how Victor was doing. He seemed to be in a much better mood so we cuddled up on the couch to watch television. About 10:00 we retired to bed.

The next day after work Rayen came to the supper table all bandaged up.

"What happened to you?" Victor asked.

"The dog bit me." She replied.

"How many times have I told you not to tease that dog? No wonder he bites."

"I'm sorry, dad. I'll be more careful."

And that was the end of that.

A few days later I wasn't even out of bed yet when I heard a huge commotion outside. I jumped out of bed and rummaged through the closet trying to find some clothes. I had no idea what was going on and I was still slightly disoriented. Before I was out of the bedroom I heard a gunshot. I came rushing out of the bedroom, tripping over some dirty clothes in the hallway. As I reached the kitchen I saw Tim come in the back door with his shotgun.

"Would you like to tell me what the hell is going on?" I asked.

"That damn dog got loose again. Rayen was on her way to catch the school bus and it cornered her. Rayen hasn't even healed up from the last attack. She was lucky that she climbed up on the stair rail and it couldn't reach her. I don't know why you and Victor keep that vicious dog anyway. What were you waiting for? Do you want it to take off her other arm?"

"What did you do?"

"I took it out back and shot it."

I was still bewildered how the dog had gotten unchained this time. Victor would be fit to be tied when he got home tonight and found out what Tim had done.

"You did what? Victor will have your hide. How dare you destroy other people's property? It wasn't yours."

"Well, you can just tell Victor whatever you want. I did what was best for everybody. Those kids are terrified of that dog. Well, they can sleep easy now knowing that it's gone."

Oh, shit would hit the fan tonight. Sally wouldn't have a boyfriend after Victor was done with him. I glared at him and Sally came in quickly from the kitchen to defend him.

"Mom, Tim just did what he thought was right. It could have been me."

She had a point there. Well, hopefully, Victor would see it that way.

I made a delicious roast beef dinner with all the trimmings. I decided to wait until after dinner to tell Victor what had happened. Jacob and Rayen dawdled by the table waiting to do the dishes.

"Run along and do your homework," I said. "I need to talk with your father."

After they left I sat back down at the table.

"Victor, something happened today.

"What else is new? There always something happening around here."

"It's about the dog."

"What did he do now?"

"I guess he chased Rayen when she went out to catch the bus."

"Did he bite her again? I told her not to tease that dog. When is she going to learn?"

He rose from the table and the vein in his temple was throbbing. I knew he was mad.

"Wait, Victor, there's more."

He sat back down.

"What."

"Well, it seems that Tim thought he was dangerous so he took it out back and shot it."

"He did what?" He stood up and strode briskly to the basement stairs.

"Tim, get your ass up here." Without waiting he went to the upstairs stairwell and yelled.

"RAYEN, get down here."

Tim appeared first with Sally hiding behind him. Rayen emerged from her bedroom about the same time.

Victor directed his attention to Tim first.

"So you think you're a big man, eh? Killing my dog."

"Victor," Tim said. "Calm down. The dog was vicious. He needed to be put down."

"And you decided you'd do it. You've got a lot of nerve."

"Daddy," Sally said. "Tim was just afraid that it might come after me. You wouldn't want that would you?"

"Get out of here the both of you. I want to talk to Rayen."

After they departed back downstairs Victor directed his attention to Rayen.

"What do you have to say for yourself?" Without waiting for a reply he continued. "I told you not to tease that dog. How many times have I told you?"

"I'm sorry, dad." She sobbed. "I didn't mean to do anything wrong."

"There was nothing wrong with that dog." He didn't say anything for a few minutes and then he finished with, "There's something wrong with you. Now go to bed and your mother will punish you tomorrow." Rayen sobbed louder and I glared at her to shut up. She quieted immediately and left to return upstairs.

I went upstairs about 8:00. Jacob and Rayen were lying on the beds reading.

I strode into the bedroom and hovered over them.

"Well, Jacob you can thank your sister for this punishment. Tomorrow is Saturday and you will spend the day weeding the garden here. When that is finished I will take you over to the other two gardens and you can weed them as well. I will come later in the afternoon to make sure you have done it right. And you better do a good job. Lights out, now." I flicked the light off as I left the room.

Good that was a job that needed doing anyway. I smiled to myself. Thanks, Tim.

Victor was still fuming when I went back downstairs.

13 KATE

Donald and Betty were coming over tonight to play cards. I had been looking forward to this all week. It was nice when we there was just the four of us. We could play Euchre. Sometimes we had two couples over and that made it a little harder.

I ran to Bentley's before the kids got home and picked up chips and pop. I made sure I picked up an extra pack of cigarettes too. I always smoked more when we had a few drinks.

Victor was bringing home a bottle of whiskey from Bancroft. I was really looking forward to a quiet evening with friends.

The children came home from school and I immediately got them to do their chores. I had soup and sandwiches on the table when they were finished.

"Take your plates downstairs. You can watch TV Make sure you bring them up and wash them before your dad gets home.

"Matilda, once Donald and Betty are here you can

come up and get a bowl of chips. Use the glasses under the bar for the pop. And make sure you kids don't make a mess O.K."

"Sure mom. Do I have to give the other kids chips and pop?"

"Yes, tonight you all get to have chips and pop." Then I directed my attention to Sally.

"Sally, do you have plans for tonight?"

"Yes, mom, I think I am going down to the restaurant. We might go to a party at Johnson's cottage later."

I hated when they went there and just hung out and I definitely hated those Johnson boys.

"O.K. will you need a ride?"

"Well you don't expect me to walk, do you? Drive me mom, and are my good jeans clean?"

"I think they're up on your bed."

"Well, I need Rayen to brush my hair."

"Fine, I'll call her. You go and get ready."

"Rayen."

Rayen appeared at the bottom of the stairs.

"Yes, mom. Come up here and help your sister get ready."

She came running up and disappeared upstairs. Sally came down a few minutes later and took off to the washroom. She looked so beautiful. Her pants looked a little too tight but I guess that's the way the kids wear them now.

She popped her head out of the bathroom.

"Where the hell is she?" she asked me.

"Don't swear honey. It's not becoming. Who Rayen?"

"Yes, Rayen. She is supposed to do my hair. Rayen. Hurry up."

"Oh hang on a minute," Matilda yelled back. "She's helping me get my pants on."

Rayen came down a few minutes later and walked

into the bathroom. I followed her. Sally was standing in front of the mirror. She handed the brush to Rayen. Sally's hair hangs down to her waist. I loved her hair. Rayen started to brush the long brown hair.

She pushed her hand against the hair to hold it.

"I said to brush it. Don't touch it. Mom, she's touching my hair. God that makes me sick." I left the bathroom without commenting.

Finally, she was ready. Victor pulled in the driveway. I already had his supper on the table.

"Come on girls. Your father's home." As Victor came in the door I gave him a kiss and put my hand out for the keys.

"Where are you off to?"

"I'm just driving Sally down to the restaurant. She is going to meet some friends there."

Don't be out too late." He warned her.

"I won't daddy."

When I returned from dropping her off Victor's dirty dishes were sitting on the table. "Rayen, come and do these damn dishes and hurry up."

"Victor, did you get the bottle."

"Yes I did but I forgot it in the trunk of the car.

"'DOLLY." I yelled.

Dolly appeared.

"Go and get the bottle out of the trunk of the car?"

She returned quickly with the bottle.

"Now you girls stay downstairs tonight. Your father and I don't want to have to listen to you. You're the oldest so make sure you keep the other ones quiet. Oh, and bring up the dirty dishes and wash them. Hurry up."

"Yes, mom."

A few minutes later she was standing washing dishes. She was just about finished when I heard Donald's truck pull into the driveway.

"Go on downstairs," I said to her.

I quickly threw my hands into the soapy water. When Donald and Betty got to the door I pulled them out, wiping them with the tea towel as I answered the door.

"Come in, come in. I'm so glad you could make it."

"Well, we just about didn't make it. Eh, Donald?"

"Yah, we just about had to cancel. Curtis is running a fever. I always worry about those fevers when they're under a year old."

"Yvette's baby-sitting. I told her to call us if he gets worse. I think he'll be O.K. though.

The fever started coming down about an hour before we left."

"Oh, well that's good. Donald, Victor's out back doing god knows what. Why don't you go back and get him."

"Sure. I'll be right back."

"Come and sit down Betty. You look tired."

"I guess a little. I was up with Curtis it must have been three times during the night. I am really looking forward to tonight. To relax and take it easy."

"That's for sure. Can I get you a drink?"

"Gingerale would be great."

"You don't want something a little stronger?"

"I don't think so. That will put me to sleep for sure."

"O.K."

I walked to the counter and pulled out two glasses. I poured a shot in one of them and then put Gingerale in both.

"We didn't catch you in the middle of dinner did we?"

"Oh know. We were finished. I was just finishing up the dishes."

"It must be hard keeping up with house work with eight of you. I know I find it hard to with just the three of us."

I lit up a cigarette.

"Yah it can be hell sometimes."

Victor and Donald came in and I got the decks of cards out of the drawer.

"I think it should be the woman against the men. What do you think Betty?"

"Well, I'm not sure. The men might get really upset if we beat them too much."

We both laughed. I sat down across from Betty and cut the cards. Donald won the cut so I got up and mixed the men each a drink.

"Gingerale or Coke," I asked.

"Coke for me."

"Gingerale, honey."

I placed their drinks down and then refreshed mine. We had only played a couple of rounds when Matilda came upstairs.

"Hi Aunt Betty, Uncle Donald. Mom, can I get some chips?"

"Sure honey, there under the cupboard. Take a bottle of pop down too."

She grabbed them and disappeared.

We continued to play cards and I kept refilling drinks. I wasn't quite sure who was winning but it was still fun. When I returned from the bathroom I overheard Victor bragging to Donald and Betty.

"Yah, she's quite the little artist. You should see some of her drawings. I would say there pretty good for a kid her age."

Betty said. "Have you thought about putting her in any classes? I know they offer them in Bancroft."

"And who might we be talking about? I asked as I sat back down.

"Victor was just telling us what a good artist Dolly is. They offer some great classes in Bancroft you might be interested in."

"Oh, I don't think so. She just does it for fun. She's

O.K. I guess." I glared at Victor. Those disgusting children were always trying to upstage my girls at every chance. There was a noticeable tension.

"Sally has been really sewing. We've been working on quilts and she really has developed a knack for it. I'm thinking we can sell tickets on one of them for the annual bazaar." I piped up to change the subject.

We played a few more hands and I noticed Betty was stifling a yawn.

"Donald, we better go home now. I'm getting really tired." She said.

"Oh sure just let me finish my drink." He chugged it back and stood up to stretch. I couldn't help but admire his physique. He was a very good-looking man. At times when he talked or the way he turned his head, he reminded me of Gary. I don't know why I always thought of him when I was drinking. Again I started feeling the same resentment for Victor. If Gary hadn't taken off when I was pregnant I would probably be married to him right now.

"Goodnight everyone," I said. Victor walked them to the door. After they left I stood up and staggered off to bed. I was asleep before my head hit the pillow.

The next day when I was cleaning up I spotted Dolly's sketching pad. I leafed through it briefly. Total rubbish. I picked it up and walked over to the stove.

I turned on the burner and debated whether I'd burn it. Oh, it would just stink up the house so I threw it in the garbage instead. Later in the afternoon Dolly looking for obviously looking for something. I knew what it was. I didn't say anything. Finally, she found it in the garbage. She pulled it out and started wiping it off.

"What are you doing?" I asked.

"Someone threw out my book."

"I did. No wonder your grades are so bad. Wasting your time doing crap like that. If you need something to do to fill your time. I'll make sure you get it. Now go out and clean out the chicken coop. After your done that come back and I'll give you something else to do."

The next day I worked the whole day cleaning and cooking. I hated when the kids had to go to school.

I was left to do everything myself. And of course I had to or Victor would know it was them doing all the work and not me. I was not impressed. Maybe I could get one of them kicked out for a few days to stay home. Hey, school was just about out. There were swimming lessons but they all didn't have to go.

Rayen had just come home from school and I put her to work right away making all the beds.

I could hear her working away upstairs. My back ached and I stopped to sit down. It wouldn't be so sore if I hadn't had to clean that stupid oven. I could have kicked myself for not remembering to get Dolly do it last night. She knew damn well it needed to be done. I always had to be after those girls. They'd be home soon. I looked at the clock in the kitchen. The bus would arrive in twenty minutes. I had already made a mental list in my mind what I wanted them to do when they got home. I had just finished my second cigarette when I heard the bus pull up. I sat there waiting for them to come in. Matilda came in first.

"Hi, honey," I said sweetly. "Did you have a good day at school?"

"Sure did mom." she came over, gave me a hug and headed straight for the bathroom.

Jacob and Dolly came in after her. I told Jacob to scrub the bathroom when Matilda came out. He didn't say anything and headed down the hall. Dolly just looked at me waiting.

"Sit down," I said.

I pointed to the chair across from me. Dolly set her books down and sat down. She looked at me with hatred.

She had a lot of nerve.

I waited until Matilda came back from the bathroom.

"Mom, did you want me to do anything for you." she asked.

"No sweetie. It's O.K. Do you have any homework?"

"Yah," she said "A little bit of math."

"Well, you run along and do it. We want to make sure you get good grades." I said. "And make sure Rayen has the beds made.

"O.K.," she said. She reached into the cupboard and grabbed a handful of cookies before retreating upstairs.

After she left I directed my attention to Dolly.

"You've been smoking drugs? Haven't you?" I said quietly.

She didn't answer.

"Answer me you filthy squaw," I demanded. I felt my voice getting louder.

She just sat there.

"What, are you deaf? Or are you just fuck'n stupid? I asked you a question and I demand an answer."

Again there was no response. I leaned over and looked her in the face. She looked right through me like I wasn't there. Well, I'd show her I was there. I leaned across the table and smacked her across the face. Her head swayed to the right from the impact but otherwise she didn't move. I got out of my chair and walked around the table and stood behind her.

"What the hell is wrong with you?" I screamed. "You're crazy. Aren't you? You stupid slut don't think you can't get away with treating me like this. No respect. I'm your mother."

I hit her across the back with my hand. I heard the echo. I stood there waiting for a reaction.

Nothing. She made me so angry. I smacked her over and over, wherever my hand connected. The back, shoulders, and head. I stopped when I realized my hand had started to sting and was throbbing. I looked her directly in the face. She looked straight ahead through me. No tears, no reaction, nothing. I was frightened for a moment and began to yell. Sally appeared and began to hit her as well. I spotted Rayen out of the corner of my eye. She was in the living room. Well maybe Dolly didn't cry but I took satisfaction from the tears streaming down her face. At least she realized what I was capable of. I put my hand in front of Sally to stop her.

Dolly finally said, "Are you done?"

I didn't answer I headed to my bedroom and sat down on my bed, cupping my injured right hand.

"Are you ok mom?" Sally asked. She had followed me and as I looked at her standing in the door frame I made a mental note to tell Victor to put a lock on our bedroom door. Dolly was really starting to scare me. I wasn't sure what she was capable of. It was so much easier when it was just Jacob and Rayen. They were so timid. I didn't feel threatened by them. I didn't like this feeling.

"I'll be fine, Sally." I just hurt my hand. It was the first time any of my girls had really jumped in to help me and that made me feel better.

I waited in the bedroom until I heard Dolly go upstairs. Then I went to the kitchen and ran my hand under cool water. The throbbing started to subside. She wouldn't get away with this. I'd get her back, that little bitch.

Victor came home and I called everyone to the table for dinner.

During dinner, I informed Victor that I had found drugs in Dolly's book bag and she was grounded for the year. She would stay home from swimming lessons and help out around the house.

14 KATE

Things were getting progressively worse around the house especially since Sally got pregnant. It had been a terrible blowout and shortly after we sent Sally away to London to an unwed mother's facility so she could get rid of it. I told everyone that she has such good grades that she had been accepted into the secretarial school. The girls were all in their teens now.

Victor was gone in the morning when I got up and never came home until I was already in bed. I had to be on those kids every day. I was losing patience. When a flyer came home from school for insurance for children I packed it safely away in my underwear drawer. Maybe that's all I needed to do.

"You will never be anything other than a whore and a prostitute like your mom," I told them constantly. "You'll be an alcoholic just like your dad." It didn't seem like I could ever tell them enough. They walked around the house like zombies, doing their cleaning and whispering to each other when they didn't think I was watching. It sickened me. Insolent stupid children.

I went for my daily trip to Bentley's for smokes and I saw a paper posted on a fence. I glanced at it casually as I walked by and then turned and ripped it down.

Sally sucks! Sally fucks! Underneath was our phone number. I was livid. I spotted two more and ran over and ripped them down as well.

People were so stupid. There is no way they knew Sally was pregnant. I was ranting and raving and then realizing how utterly ridiculous I sounded even to myself I stormed into the store for my smokes. I glared at Trina behind the counter. "Did you see who put these up?" I yelled at here shaking the papers in my hand. She shook her head no. "Give me a pack of Peter Jackson." She set them on the counter and I grabbed them and walked out. I didn't realize until halfway home that I forgot to pay for them.

I would string someone up for this.

I was screaming before I even walked in the door. "Do any of you little fucks know who put these signs up?"

I heard the kids come running. I lined them all up in the kitchen. Matilda read the crumpled paper and started to cry. "OMG god mom where did you get these? I hate those boys. I can never leave the house again." She ran to her room and I heard her throw herself on her bed.

"I'm sure you're sisters or brother had something to do with it, didn't you?" I demanded.

"No mom, I've never seen them before," Jacob said, Rayen stood with her head down and Dolly had a guilty look on her face.

"Line up! Rayen, get me the strap." Rayen backed up but didn't go towards the drawer.

"I said Rayon, get me the strap and you better listen." She ran to the drawer to get it and handed it to me.

I gave the three of them the strap. Anytime I heard a whimper they got another one.

"Go to your room and don't come out until I tell you."

And so as each day passed, it was worse than the last. Jacob and Rayen barely spoke at all and Dolly quit speaking completely. In fact, the only one she spoke to was Jacob and Rayen. If I asked her a question she ignored me. I didn't punish her. At seventeen, she was now the size of a full grown woman. I knew that something was about to erupt and I started to fear for Victor and my safety. Victor had put the lock on the bedroom door but it didn't give me much solace. I started to sleep less and less each night and reverted to taking naps through the day.

Dolly came home from school and I sensed something was different. She went directly upstairs and I heard her rummaging around. I snuck upstairs to see what she was doing. I peeked through the crack in the door and I saw her pulling clothes off hangers and throwing it on the bed. Then she turned to empty out her dresser drawer. I walked into the room but I didn't say anything. She continued with what she was doing. Finally, I said.

"What are you doing?"

"Packing," she replied.

Finally! She was finally going to be out of my life for good. I walked over and started to help her.

"Do you know where you're going?"

"Yes."

We finished in silence and I watched as she carried her bags downstairs. For a brief second, I panicked. Her cheque wouldn't be coming. Then with relief I realized. No one needs to know that she's not here. I'm not going to tell anyone. I had put up with enough shit from her and these other two, all these years. I deserved those cheques. I'd continue cashing them until someone questioned it. If they did I'd feign ignorance.

I went downstairs to make supper. Dolly didn't come down to join us for supper but about 7:00 she came down and made a phone call. I stayed in the kitchen so I could hear what she was saying.

"Can you store my stuff for a while?"

She didn't talk for a while and I assumed it was her father she was speaking to. The only other thing she said was "Toronto." It was sure hard to follow what was going on with this one-sided conversation. After she completed her call she returned back upstairs. I didn't see her for the rest of the weekend. Victor went up to speak to her on Saturday evening. I sat on the stairs so I could hear what was going on.

"Did you say anything?" he asked.

There was no answer.

"I asked you a question. Did you say anything?"

"No, I didn't say anything."

"Where are you going to go? Have you thought about that?"

No answer again. I heard Victor moving towards the door so I ran quickly down the stairs and sat on the couch. Victor came downstairs and went out slamming the door, as usual. I didn't see him again until he banged on our bedroom door in the wee hours of the morning. I had locked it. I had even gone so far so to barricade the bedroom closet. In case she tried to crawl through from the coat closet. I was sure that she would try to do something to me. I wasn't exactly sure what. I let him in and crawled back into bed.

I didn't have to worry about Dolly, she stayed upstairs the rest of the weekend except to come down to use the bathroom. She didn't speak to anyone. On Saturday I watched Jacob make a sandwich and grab an apple. I didn't say anything. On Monday morning I peered through the curtains to watch her carry her suitcases out to catch the school bus. That would be the last I would see of her until Christmas, eight months later. I felt an overwhelming feeling of peace. Now to get rid of those other two.

Victor's sister's boys, Walter and Terry, were visiting from Hamilton. Victor's sister, Rita had come to visit for a few days and had decided to continue her visit in Peterborough leaving the boys with us. The boys would be staying with us for an additional week. I had only been awake for a short while. Victor had woke me up to have coffee with him before he went down to work on Peter's farm. I could hear noises upstairs like people were rolling around on the floor.

"Kate will you go up there and tell those kids to take it easy or they'll be coming through that ceiling."

Victor never disciplined those kids. I don't know why he couldn't go up there and tell them to be quiet himself. I had to do everything. I was in a foul mood anyway. Sally was back home now and she had tried to sneak in about 2:00 a.m. and had managed to wake me up in the process. She was drunk and had fallen over the corner of the couch which had woken me up. I told her if she wasn't more careful her dad would catch her. She was lucky it wasn't her dad who had woken up or he would have tanned her hide. I was concerned she would get pregnant again but Sally assured me she would be careful. I hadn't been able to sleep after that and had been awake until about 4:00. I pushed my chair back and went upstairs to do his bidding. Terry and Jacob were wrestling around on the floor. Matilda was sitting on the side of the bed cheering them on.

"Hey, you too, be quiet. Sally is trying to sleep. Like anyone can sleep in this house."

They immediately stopped.

"Sorry Aunt Kate," Terry said. Jacob didn't say

anything but I was sure I saw him smirk. That little bastard. I went back downstairs. As I sat down at the table I stubbed my toe on the table leg and cursed.

"What's wrong, honey?"

Without thinking I said.

"Jacob hit me."

Victor was upstairs within seconds. I'm sure he must have taken the stairs two at a time. He didn't normally go upstairs so I was quite surprised. I jumped up quickly to follow him. I'd never seen him quite this upset. I was thoroughly enjoying this. I got upstairs in time to watch him grab Jacob and throw him against the wall. Jacob slid down to the floor.

"And stay up here." he said.

Then he turned and brushed past me and went back downstairs. I immediately followed him.

Wow, he must love me. I was never really sure anymore.

"He's never done that before, has he, Kate?"

"No. He hasn't."

Shortly after Terry wandered downstairs. He stood around for a few minutes in the kitchen.

He just stood there standing on one foot, and then the other. Victor looked at him and finally said. "Well if you want to say something spit it out."

"What did Jacob do?"

"You were up there. You know what he did. He hit Kate. I won't let any of these kids get away with a stunt like that."

"When?" Terry asked surprised.

"A few minutes ago when Kate was upstairs."

"No, he didn't," Terry said. "Aunt Kate told us to be quiet and we said O.K. That was it. Jacob didn't hit her."

Oh shit, I thought. I better think of something to cover my butt. The vein in Victor's temple looked like it was going to pop it was throbbing so hard. I knew he was really mad.

Victor walked to the bottom of the stairs and yelled. "You can come down now, Jacob."

He glared at me but he didn't say anything. He just went out. I knew he would. That's how he dealt with everything.

I was so happy when Rita finally came back to get her boys. I hated having anyone around the house.

With the new school year starting, we were busy getting the school cleaning completed. My back was sore and the kids were getting bigger, which made it harder to beat them. I was annoyed that Dolly was gone and I had to do more of the work. Dolly had been doing most of the cooking. I made her and Jacob, do the heaviest jobs. Jacob was still just a straggly, long and lanky bastard. It made my life harder only having two of them to work. Jacob was in high school now with Matilda and Rayen was the only one left at the elementary school. Jacob and Rayen were different now that Dolly was gone. They seemed more defiant and the more I hit them it was like it didn't seem to make a difference.

We continued to clean the school every night. It took longer with just Jacob, Rayen and I.

I would strap Jacob and tell him it was because of something that Rayen did and strap Rayen before Jacob got home from school and tell her it was because of Jacob. I would listen to Rayen and Jacob arguing and I was quite pleased. Victor kept bugging me about Rayen and Jacob sharing a room but there was no way in hell they were bunking with my girls.

Rayen was spending a lot of time away babysitting so she was able to buy some of her own clothes now. I wasn't spending any of my money on her. Jacob spent more time helping Victor in the evenings with the trapping which just meant I had to do the majority of the work.

I really didn't like that new teacher Rayen had this year. He seemed to be spending a lot of time with her and I wasn't pleased. I wasn't pleased at all, and now I heard that stupid teacher had brought a counselor to talk to Rayen. I had received this information from Father Ginelli. I would have to find out what she told him.

That Mr. Keller was just trying to make trouble. Well, I'd make sure he didn't make anymore. Rayen had been walking around dreamy eyed all the time. This happening mostly when she talked about him. I should have caught on sooner. Now I knew what she was up to. I would speak to her at supper tonight.

Victor arrived home from work at 5:00 and I put supper on the table.

"Come and eat," I yelled.

The kids clamored to the table and sat down. Matilda grabbed a piece of cheese off the plate and I slapped her lightly on the hand.

"Not until we say grace," I said.

I bowed my head and said. "Dear Lord. Thank you for the food we are about to receive.

Amen."

"Amen." was echoed in unison.

We made idle small talk. I was picking at my food waiting patiently for the right time to broach the subject. Rayen nonchalantly passed me the mashed potatoes and said.

"Mr. Keller would like me to babysit for them on Friday. Is it O.K.?"

She was flaunting it. I couldn't believe it. She had just had her thirteenth birthday a couple of months prior. I knew those kids would grow up to be nothing but tramps.

"Oh I'm sure he does and the answer is No. You're not babysitting for them. I know what you've been up to.

You're sleeping with him. Aren't you?"

Rayen just sat there trying to look innocent. I knew she wasn't innocent.

Victor said quietly. "Kate, leave her alone."

I glared at him. He stood up and walked downstairs. As if on cue, the rest of the kids followed him. Then I directed my attention back to Rayen.

"Answer me."

"No. No, I'm not. I didn't do anything." Rayen said crying.

"Don't lie to me." I threatened. "Well, I wonder what his wife will think when I let her know what you've been up to. Then I bet she won't want you babysitting or doing anything else for that matter. You're nothing but a little slut. You and your sister. You'll never turn out to be anything."

I walked over and yanked the phone off the hook.

"No mom, please. I didn't do anything."

I quickly dialed the Keller's number that I had memorized earlier. I was in luck. A female answered at the other end.

"Hello, Mrs. Keller," I asked.

"Yes it is." was the reply.

"This is Mrs. Gabbon, Rayen's mother."

"Oh yes, hello. It's nice to hear from you."

"Well, I don't think you'll find it so nice when you find out why I'm calling."

"Oh, is there something wrong?" she said with concern.

"I just wanted you to know that my daughter has been sleeping with your husband." I waited for a second for a response but there was none. "I thought you should know."

"I'm sure you're mistaken. My husband is not like that and frankly Mrs. Gabbon, I don't think I want to continue this conversation with you."

"Fine but you keep your husband away from my daughter. And she won't be babysitting for you anymore and she won't be going on the school field trip to see the Parliament buildings. She's already learned more than enough from your husband. In fact, you can just mail her report card. She won't be returning to school at all."

With this finished, I hung up. Rayen was sitting at the table crying. Sure she was crying now. Now that she got caught. I knew she had to be doing something to get those good grades. Well, I showed that little slut. And she thought she could get away with it.

"Quit crying and do these dishes. As soon as you're done, go to bed. I don't want to see you again tonight."

I left her in the kitchen and went down to watch television with the kids and Victor. Victor didn't mention the incident at all. He was learning.

I was sitting enjoying my morning coffee the next day when I heard a noise upstairs. I walked quietly upstairs and I saw a person lying in bed. I knew it was Jacob or Rayen. It had to be Jacob. I went back downstairs and grabbed the belt out of the drawer. That lazy bastard hadn't gone to school. I went back upstairs and walked directly over to the bed. I pulled the covers back and started swinging. I'll show him. I wasn't sure who exactly it was until he turned around.

I started yelling. "You lazy prick. Do you think you're so smart that you don't have to go to school? You're a good for nothin' half-breed."

He tried to say something but I continued to yell. I didn't want to hear anything he had to say. The belt swung around his arm and dug in. Shit that would leave a mark and I was always so careful. This made me even madder. I kept swinging until I was too tired to hit him anymore. Jacob was crying and he finally said through sobs.

"I didn't have any school today. I wrote all my

exams."

I sat there for a few minutes and then I said.

"You are supposed to be a man. Look at you crying like a baby. You are just like your father. Good for absolutely nothing. Get your ass out of bed and cut the lawn."

That should take him at least the rest of the morning. I'd find him something else to do this afternoon. We had planned on going camping this weekend so he could get everything ready. That would keep him busy.

That night with the truck packed we took off to the lake. It was quite dark when we arrived at Algonquin Park. Davey and Annette were already waiting for us there. We found our spot and everyone pitched in. Soon the tents were up and after a bonfire, we all retired to sleep.

I woke up the next morning about 8:00am and the sun was stifling. I crawled out of the tent and peered quickly around to see if I could see Victor or the kids. Annette and Davey had their tent right beside ours and I saw Annette grabbing the coffee pot off of the Coleman stove.

"I hope you made enough for me," I said. She looked over and laughed. I must have looked funny as I crawled out trying not to get tangled in the poles and rope.

"Sure did, and breakfast too. Make it snappy before Davey eats it all."

She handed me a black coffee as I approached her.

"Where are the kids?"

"Do you even have to ask? Swimming of course. Did you sleep well?"

"Great. I love being out here, Annette. It's so fresh."

"Sure beats city life that's for sure."

"I guess I'd feel that way too if I lived in the city."

"Now let's not get into that again Kate. We went down that road last night."

I remembered. I always got so irritated with my life after I'd had a few. It was had been fun sitting around the campfire singing, though. Victor showed up and gave me a hug.

"Hi, sleepyhead."

"Morning hon," I said.

"Davey and I have been out fishing for hours already. We thought we'd come back for breakfast and then we're heading back out. Where are the kids?"

"Annette says they're swimming. Did you catch anything?"

"Can't you smell it? We're having five rainbow trout for breakfast. And of course, I caught the biggest one."

"Yah right Victor. Don't let him fool you, girls. I caught the biggest one." Davey said winking at me.

We sat around the fire idly chit-chatting and eating. Victor and Davey got up to get ready to head out fishing again when Sally came running up to us.

"Rayen's running around the beach with no bathing suit." She said.

"What?" Victor said standing up.

"She's naked and she's running around the beach."

Victor took off at a run. I could see him loosening his belt as he went. The beach was approximately 4 city blocks away. I started to chase after him but Annette called me back.

"Let Victor handle it, Kate. You don't need the aggravation." She said. I returned to the fire and waited. My head was pounding from the activities the night before. It didn't take long and I could hear Victor screaming and Rayen crying. I watched as Victor appeared at the top of the hill. He was pulling Rayen with one hand and hitting her with his belt with the other. I thought she was still naked and ran with a blanket to cover her. As I ran up to them I realized that Rayen had on the peach-colored two-piece bathing suit that we had bought at the Madonna House.

"Victor, wait until we get back to the camp. Everyone is watching."

"I don't give a shit if they're watching. I won't have my daughter acting like a two-bit whore. I have told those girls over and over. Keep your god damn pants on. Why doesn't anyone ever listen?"

Rayen was attempting to defend herself.

"I didn't do anything."

"Shut up, Rayen," I said. "You're just making matters worse."

And so as per usual. Our trip was ruined and we packed up our stuff and went home. Those kids ruined everything.

15 KATE

"Rayen, go down and vacuum the basement and then rake the carpet."

I loved that red shag carpet. It sure made the rec-room look great. In fact, the whole house was looking pretty good. The bank account was growing. If only I didn't have to put up with those kids. I heard Rayen go down to the basement.

"Jacob, when you're done those dishes, go and feed the animals."

I went to the bedroom to lay down. I don't know why I was so tired these days. Of course, anyone would be tired chasing after these kids all day. I heard the vacuum turn off and Rayen came upstairs. I walked out from the bedroom and watched as she disappeared around the corner.

"Rayen, did you rake the rug?"

"Oh, I'm sorry mom. I forgot. I'll go down and do it now." As she walked back towards the basement stairs. I grabbed her by the shoulder and spun her around.

"You are so stupid. Can't you do anything right?"

"Mom, I said I'd do it. I'm sorry. I forgot."

"Oh yeah, you conveniently forget everything. Don't talk back to me. You get your ass to that school and I want you to clean the whole thing. I'll come down later and if you forget to do anything, anything, you'll really get it. And I mean it. You'll never forget anything ever again. I don't care if it takes you all night. You're going to do it."

As usual, Rayen started to cry.

There is something seriously wrong with that kid. All she ever does is cry. Christ, she's fourteen. You'd think she'd grow up. I watched her as she grabbed her shoes and stood by the door.

"What, do you think I'm going to drive you? I don't think so. You can walk. Now move it."

The screen door slammed and I watched her as she walked down the driveway. Lassie followed her. That dog was always following her. Good, with any luck someone would hit that mutt. Victor was always bringing home something to give me more work to do. Like I didn't have enough already. About an hour later Victor came home.

"You haven't looked out the window lately, have you, Kate? Call the kids and tell them to help me round up those damn chickens. They're all over the yard."

I yelled for Matilda and Jacob.

"Where's Rayen? She can help too."

"She's at the school."

"Oh, sports or something?"

"No, she was talking back to me so I sent her there to clean it."

"By herself?"

"Yah, she's a big girl," I said defensively.

"Did you drive her there and unlock the door?"

Shit, I hadn't thought of that. She wouldn't be able to get in.

"No, I told her to walk."

"I'll go and get her. Kate, sometimes you don't think. Do you?"

He grabbed the car keys and I heard him pull out of the driveway. He returned within minutes.

"She's not there."

"Well, I don't know where she would have gone."

Victor stormed off to the car again. I ran after him.

"Where are you going?

"Where do you think I'm going? I'm going to find her."

With that, he drove away and left me standing there.

He returned again about an hour later and walked into the house.

He sat down at the table.

"She's not coming back." He said in a low voice. It was like a slap in the face. This couldn't be happening. I'd already spent at least two months of government cheques that hadn't even come in yet.

"What do you mean she's not coming back? You found her?"

"Yah, I ran into Tony Smitty at the restaurant and he told me that he drove her down to Gary's camp. I drove down to the camp and she was there."

"Well, why didn't you bring her home then? What, do you want me to do it?" I quizzed him.

"No, I don't want you to do it. I don't know what the hell she told Gary. You've really messed up, this time, Kate. Gary and I got into a huge fight. He says he's not going to make her come back."

"There was nothing else I could do so I left. What the hell brought this on anyway?"

I sat down at the table and started to cry. I figured a few tears might bring some sympathy.

"I don't know Victor she's started talking back and she won't do anything I say. I don't know what's got into her. It wasn't anything I did."

It's not bad enough the way people were already talking about us. Have you any idea what they'll think now. What there saying."

"Well, they can think whatever they want. We're not that bad. Jacob is still here, isn't he?"

"Yah, but for how long? If it wasn't for us, nobody would have anything to gossip about."

He walked outside and slammed the door.

Sally and Tim came home just before supper. I should have known. Where there was food, there was Tim. They were supposed to be spending the weekend with his parents in Bancroft so I was quite surprised when they showed up. I set a couple extra plates at the dinner table and sent Tim out to get Victor for supper. We were just having grill cheese and tomato soup so I was able to make more easily. When they returned we all sat down to eat.

I was just waiting for Tim to open his big mouth. He always did. After he'd filled it for at least a half an hour he said.

"Where's Rayen?"

I glared at him.

"She's gone. Victor and I decided we couldn't handle her anymore so we sent her to stay with her dad." I glanced at Victor. He didn't say anything but he glared back. I wasn't sure if Tim had seen our interaction but he didn't pursue it.

"Oh." was all he said.

"Thank-god," Matilda said. "Now I'll have my own bed. Maybe I'll have my room back soon too." as she looked at Jacob.

"Shut up Matilda," Victor said as he pushed his plate away. I was surprised. He wasn't usually gruff with our children.

A couple day later Jacob didn't return home. No one

said a word about it.

The cheques continued to arrive in the mail. And just like with Dolly, I continued to cash them.

No one checked in on them when they were here so why would they check on them now. And the best part of all was that I didn't have to deal with them anymore. It was finally over. I smiled.

16 MARIA

I received a call from Dolly, right out of the blue. I was speechless. I had so much to say but absolutely no words. There was a hesitation before a quiet voice said.

"Is this Maria Watchtower? Maria Paul?

"Yes," I said tentatively. I couldn't dare wish or believe who might be on the other end of the line or I might jinx it and they would hang up.

"Mom, it's me, Dolly." And then we were both crying and sobbing so hard that neither of us could continue.

"I'll call you back." She said and I heard the dial tone in my ear.

Could it really be? Or was someone playing a cruel joke on me? "Matt, Matt," I screamed and ran out of the house. Matt was in the backyard tending to the chickens. "Matt, come quick," I yelled. I didn't dare leave the porch in case I missed the phone. It had been nearly 30 years since I had seen my girls.

"Dolly called me." I blurted out excitedly. "She's going to call me back. I cried and laughed and paced back and forth across the kitchen as I watched the phone. Matt sat on the chair with a big smile. Finally, it rang. After an awkward introduction, I listened as Dolly explained that her and Rayen were living in Calgary. Five hours away. Jacob was living in Ontario. None of the other kids knew that Dolly was looking for me. We made plans for Matt and I to travel to Calgary the following day. She told me she was living in a condo and had two daughters and a huge Rottweiler. She didn't want me to be frightened of her puppy when we got there.

I had no idea what to wear and I tried on a zillion outfits before I settled on a purple shirt with matching skirt. I had worn that outfit to my cousin's wedding and it made me feel pretty. I was nonstop chatter until we arrived in Calgary. We found Dolly's place easy enough. As we pulled up out front of her place I fixed my hair and put some lipstick on. "Do I look ok?" I asked Matt. "You look beautiful Maria. Now go and meet your daughter. She will love you, don't worry," as he patted my hand for reassurance. He stayed in the truck and I made my way slowly to her door. What would I say? What would I do?

The door opened before I reached it and my daughter, Dolly came out on the step. Her arms were open and I went into them. After all the years I had cried, I still had lots more that were flooding out.

"Come in Mom." I had heard this from my foster children many times throughout the years but this was different. This was my daughter, my oldest daughter.

"Is that your husband mom?

In my excitement, I had forgotten he was there. 'Yes, yes it is." I smiled. "His name is Matt, I'll go get him."

The house was beautiful and clean and smelled

heavenly. Dolly had prepared a wonderful roast dinner with all the trimmings. As we both talked nonstop, Matt and I sat at the table while Dolly's children set the table and brought all the food.

My granddaughters, Jenny and Val were so young. Jenny looked about 12 and Val about 8. They looked at me shyly throughout dinner. I think they were impressed that they were meeting their grandmother. All I could do was smile. No, I was beaming. I had grandchildren.

After dinner, I helped clear the table but Dolly would not let me help with dishes and we continued to talk. "Does Rayen live close to you? I asked. Dolly promptly went to the bedroom to make a phone call. She had a funny look on her face when she came back.

"I don't think Rayen can come today." She said.

My eyebrows lifted involuntarily. "Oh, oh ok, that's ok," and my heart sank.

"Mom, you have to understand. We heard terrible, terrible things about you all while we grew up. You and dad. Rayen just needs some time. I think she may be in shock. She's only about 5 minutes away so if I don't hear from her I'll go check on her later."

This was the first I was hearing anything about where my children were or how they grew up.

"Oh, she didn't know I was coming."

"No mom, I figured I'd wait until you were really here." After a moment she continued. "We've had a lot of disappointment in our life mom."

I wanted to hear more but she went quiet. I sensed my daughter was extremely sad and I had no idea why.

A while later there was a knock on the door.

Dolly's face brightened and she smiled, "She did come. I'll go let her in."

They talked for a few minutes at the door before they came up to see me. Dolly stepped aside and behind her stood my baby. She was a woman now. The sparkling eyes that I remembered, though, throughout the years were gone and I could see she had been crying. She was shy and distant and stayed for a short time.

Dolly and I talked into the wee hours of the night and it became clear to me why my girls, I had just met, acted the way they did. I had prayed for happiness and peace for all my children but as my daughter, Dolly described the horrors of what they had lived through all I could do was cry. I was ready to jump on a plane to Ontario myself. That horrible, despicable woman had terrorized my children for years and I hated her. I didn't know her but I hated her. It sickened me and I was so angry. Dolly knew how agitated I was becoming so she said, "Mom remember when you took us to the powwow. I can't remember where we were and Jacob and I danced."

"Oh my god, my girl that was such a good day. Your dad was so proud. You and Jacob both won ribbons and prize money. I had such a sore back. I was pregnant with Rayen. We went home and you guys kept at me and kept at me. I was so tired but you finally got your way and I made fry bannock."

"We had such good times then," Dolly said. "Remember the night it was so cold and Jacob and I didn't want our horse to freeze so we bugged you and bugged you until you let us put him in the kitchen and then dad came home and it was so dark and he tripped over him or the horse kicked him or something." We both laughed and told stories for hours. It was starting to get light before we finally made our way to our beds. Neither of us wanted the night to end.

Even when I laid down beside Matt I couldn't sleep. I still needed to see Jacob, and he was so far away. Oh, I hope Rayen smiles for me when I see her again. I knew how she felt. We were virtually strangers but she would grow to love me as I had loved her and all my children through all these years. I felt a closeness to Dolly. I wondered if Jacob would remember me too. I was still in awe of the whole situation and all I could think was, this is really happening.

I thought of the monster that had raised my children. I should have helped them. I should have gone to Ontario. I had no way of knowing but I should have known. I thought all the pain I was feeling through the years was my own pain. Now I realized that it had been my children's pain as well. There was nothing I could do to take back those years so I needed to look forward. I needed to enjoy the time that we had together now, as a family.

In a whirlwind of activities, we arranged a reunion of all my children in Thunderchild First Nation reserve. Matt and I returned home after a wonderful meeting with my two daughters and I anxiously awaited the reunion. Jacob would be driving from Ontario to attend our annual powwow. Dawn Blaus, a reporter from Windspeaker called me a number of times and interviewed me over the phone. They made arrangements to meet us at the Thunderchild Powwow to write a story.

It seemed to take forever but finally the day was upon us. Dolly drove to our house in Kehewin and a bunch of us drove to the Thunderchild Powwow. It was only a 2-hour drive.

Once we arrived in Turtleford I asked Matt to stop at the drugstore. The stomach pains I had been experiencing for quite a while now were progressively getting worse. I ran in and bought tums. Nothing was going to ruin this day.

I chewed the antacids nervous and excited. Would Jacob recognize me? Would he like me? Would he be unsure like Rayen? Would he blame me for what happened like Rayen did? So many questions raced through my mind on the short drive from Turtleford to my reserve, the Thunderchild First Nation reserve. I had only spoken to Jacob once on the phone. It was an awkward conversation as we both struggled to get through it. Amidst the weeping I did learn that he was living in Ontario, he was single and he had become a welder. Both he and Rayen seemed to be struggling with alcohol but Dolly as always remained independent and resourceful. I could see the anger she carried but she was proud. I admired her strength raising her two girls on her own. Rayen had two daughters as well. I hadn't met her husband or her daughters yet. I wonder how many would be here today.

Finally, we were on the grounds. I could hear the drums as I got out of the car. The drumming always made me feel at peace. Today would be the first time I was with all my children in just about 30 years. As I felt another sharp pain in my groin I put a big smile on my face and jumped out of the truck.

I spotted Dolly right away. She motioned for us to bring our truck over beside her car. Rayen had already arrived in her car. It was an older gray sedan and she climbed out and opened the passenger door for a pretty little girl. She looked to be about 8 or 9.

As I walked over to them Rayen brought her daughter over to meet me.

"Mom, this is my daughter Nikita. Nikita, this is your grandmother." Another granddaughter. I not only had my children back but I had grandchildren as well. It really was a perfect day. Nikita was shy but she came and shook my hand.

Aww, what a polite little girl. I smiled down at her and said. "Oh my goodness, you are such a pretty little girl, Nikita. I'm your grandmother." She smiled back and ran over to play with Jenny and Val. "Have you seen your brother Jacob yet? I asked Rayen.

"Not yet, Mom but I just got a text." She glanced at

her phone. As she was texting she said, "Mom he's in Turtleford by the drugstore. He's lost. I will go get him and he can follow me in. We'll be right back."

Rayen gave me a quick hug. "Nikita stay and play with Jenny and Val. Don't take off by yourself." and then my daughter was gone.

I hadn't been home to Thunderchild for a long, long time and everywhere I looked were relatives coming up, shaking my hand, hugging me and everything seemed like a blur. Dolly never left my side and I introduced her to as many people as I saw. Finally, she pulled me aside and said, "Mom I will never remember all of these people. Are they all our family?"

I hugged her close and said. "Yes, they are all your family, my girl, and there are still so many more to meet.

Just then Dolly said, "Mom, Rayen and Jacob just pulled in. I felt like I would faint and I followed her as we made our way through the crowd.

I started to weep before we made it to the cars. Jacob stood tall. His hair was cut short and he stood at least a foot taller than Rayen. He was handsome and even though so many years had passed I could still see my baby Jacob in his face. My children, all of them, standing in front of me.

I held out my arms and just cried as I held them.

Then we were all talking at once and laughing and crying. I thought this day would never come. I had dreamed of this very moment for years. I had the biggest smile and I was at peace. Finally, I was at peace.

The MC started calling out over the PA, "It is a very special day today at the Thunderchild First Nation reserve. We are having a 30-year reunion today. A reunion way overdue. Windspeaker is here to cover this amazing story. Our very own Maria Paul and her children are here today. Can we have a warm welcome for Maria Paul and her children? Can Maria and her children make their way to the stage? Maria Paul, Dolly, Jacob and Rayen please make your way to the stage."

As we made our way to the stage he continued speaking over the PA system. "Today we will play a song in honor of this great event. 1993 Annual Powwow and we have a 30-year reunion of mother and children."

We stood on that stage as the reserve applauded and I was so distracted I don't even know what song they were singing. I just knew this was the happiest day of my life.

One the song was over we made our way off the stage and the reporter from Windspeaker came and interviewed each of us. It was all kind of a blur but I do remember saying,

"The Creator answered all my prayers," I told her. "Today I'm happy," and

"I feel great. It's been a long time. "I've been hurt too long. This is my happiest day."

Once we were finished speaking with the reporter we found Matt who had found a seat on the bleachers. He had saved a few seats so I introduced him to Jacob. They hit it off right away. Matt took lots of pictures of us and we stayed for the full day enjoying the dancing, music, and relatives. Towards evening I was getting extremely tired with all the excitement. We decided to all make our way back to our home in Kehewin.

We had a caravan of vehicles. We went first in our truck because we knew all the shortcuts. Then Dolly's car followed with Jenny and Val, Rayen with Nikita was next in her car, followed by Jacob. It took us about 3 hours to make the trip back home and I was so thankful I made sure all of the bedrooms were ready for them.

It was so nice to have all my children and grandchildren in the same house. We have a big four bedroom house so each of the children had their own room and the grandchildren made up beds in the living room.

The next few days were filled with tours around the reserve and picnics and barbecues. My grandchildren loved playing with our three dogs and running to the store for treats. We made home movies and spent hours just talking and getting to know each other.

I still felt a distance between Rayen, Jacob and me and I tried my hardest to make them feel welcome. Dolly was a great cook and helped me with meals. It really started to feel like we were a family.

After my grandchildren went to sleep we would sit around the kitchen table and we would talk. Just talk and take turns telling stories. My children were so close and I was so grateful that they had each other and had survived their terrible ordeal. Twelve years was even longer than the time I had spent in prison. My children explained in horrific detail all the abuse they had endured by their aunt and it broke my heart.

I could understand their resistance in meeting me now. I couldn't believe they hadn't received even one of my letters. They should have been returned to Thunderchild so many years ago. That was their home. That was their right. None of what happened made any sense.

"Dolly do you have that aunt's phone number?" I asked. Dolly wrote it down on a piece of paper. As I dialed the phone number my hands trembled because I was so angry.

The phone rang three times and I was beginning to wonder if it would be answered and then I finally heard an unfamiliar voice say "Hello."

I couldn't speak for a moment and then as my children watched me, I said. "Is this Kate Gabbon?"

"Yes, it is." Was the answer.

"This is Maria Paul-Watchtower. I have my children here with me and I just want you to know, that I know what you did, and if I ever get my hands on you. I'll break your fukn neck."

I slammed the phone down and I was overwhelmed by the emotion that coursed through my veins. I hadn't been able to help my children. I should have been able to help them. I felt so guilty but as my children hugged me now, I felt a tiny bit of satisfaction.

"Did she get charged?" I asked.

"No mom she didn't get charged or nothing," Dolly said. "She got away with it. All of it. We have tried for years to get someone to charge her, or put her in jail but no one will help us." She shook her head in disgust, "No one cares mom. We tried to get the Bancroft OPP to charge her and I just got a letter a few months back from the Assistant District Attorney. Evidently, it's not in the people's interest to charge her. Whatever the hell that means."

Jacob blurted out, "But we're not going to stop trying mom. What she did was so wrong and it was a crime." Rayen immediately started to cry and she took off to the bathroom.

"Will she be ok?" I asked the other two.

"We'll never really be ok mom. We're different now. Going through what we went through changes you. Rayen doesn't talk about it. She'll be ok in a bit."

I shook my head in disgust and I felt so helpless. The same way I had felt most of my life. Everything always so out of control. Someone else always making the decisions.

Before I knew it the week was up and the girls were returning to Calgary. Jacob would be going home and I didn't want to say goodbye. It just wasn't enough time with them. We made promises to see each other as often as we could. I knew they had to go back to their jobs and their lives but it tore at my heart strings and I couldn't hold back the tears as I watched them pull out of our driveway.

Johnny had gotten out of jail shortly after the reunion and came to stay with Matt and I. So our lives became very hectic trying to keep up with all the children.

I phoned Jacob every Saturday and I called Dolly and Rayen every Sunday. Matt and I made the trip to Calgary at least once a month alternating between Dolly and Rayen's house. Sometimes Johnny would come with us but normally he was attending Karate Competitions. He had so many trophies and he had won so much money competing. It made me smile. That was one area where he was extremely focused.

I looked forward to the weekends and once in a while, we would go to Calgary during the week. I got to see Dolly's office at Indian Oil & Gas Canada and Rayen's office at Petro Canada. I was so proud of my children. All of my children. I didn't get to see Jacob and I wished that he lived closer. He spent a lot of time in Fort McMurray with his welding job.

The pain in my abdomen was getting progressively worse. Matt insisted I go to the doctor but I was sure it would pass. I wanted to spend as much time as I could with my children.

It was Thursday evening and we were all packed to make our weekend trip to Calgary on Friday. I was having trouble sleeping these days because of the pain but tonight I had dozed off about 9pm. Matt and I had sat on the porch swing watching the northern lights all evening as they danced across the sky. They were mesmerizing and I had become terribly sleepy.

I closed my eyes and drifted into a troubled sleep. Lights were flashing before my eyes and I tried to run. I struggled as I felt the tightening of its hold on me pulling me down further and further. The drumming was deafening and I was all alone. Then the dream changed drastically and it was very different. Instead of continuing to pull me down it started to choke me and I couldn't breathe at all and then excruciating pain shot through me with such force I couldn't bear it, and I screamed out in pain.

Matt picked me up out of our bed, carried me to the truck and rushed me to the hospital. We sat in emergency in Bonnyville for what seemed like hours. They finally gave me a shot of Toradol which made the pain bearable. After seeing the emergency doctor and getting poked and prodded, I was admitted to hospital. They continued to run a whole series of tests and they wouldn't let me go home. I didn't want Matt to leave me but he came the following morning and stayed with me all day. "Do you want me to phone the kids?" he asked me.

"No, I don't want them to worry." And then I remembered what day it was. "Oh, yes phone Dolly and tell her we can't make it this weekend," I told him. It had only been two years since the reunion and I didn't want my kids worrying about me.

"I'll be out of here before you know it," I told him. "I miss cuddling with you, Matt. I just want to come home."

"Oh Maria, I miss you too. I just want you home but I want you to be well." Matt kissed me on the forehead before he left.

The next morning a doctor I didn't recognize came in to talk to me.

"Maria, we need to send you to Edmonton. We have found some abnormalities in your blood work and we need to send you to a specialist. He is the best in his field. We need to send you right away. You'll go by ambulance within the hour. I've made all the arrangements. You need to let your family know."

As he walked out of the room I thought he must have made a mistake. I have a bit of pain but I'm fine. This was not what I wanted to hear. I rang for the nurse and she came right away.

"I need to phone my husband, Matt Watchtower," I told her.

She brought me a phone and as it was ringing I still couldn't believe what I had just been told. Matt answered on the second ring.

"Matt they're sending me to Edmonton in the ambulance. I'm not sure what's going on. Can you come? Maybe pack me a bag with pajamas and my toothbrush and stuff."

Matt arrived within a half hour and I heard them tell him he could follow the ambulance to the Royal Alexander Hospital in Edmonton. I was already loaded on a stretcher.

The nurse had brought something and put it in my IV and I was so drugged and everything was very foggy but I had no pain.

I woke up in a different hospital room and Matt was there. I tried to talk to him but the words I heard in my head were garbled and I could not make them come out right. I drifted in and out of consciousness but every time I looked, Matt was with me. He would be there sitting in the chair, or holding my hand and sometimes he was beside me crying.

I heard him say, "You're at the Royal Alexander Hospital, Maria. I've called the kids for you."

I didn't understand why Matt had called the children. I was really confused and I was finding it hard to breathe. As I gasped for air I tried to ask Matt what was going on but the words wouldn't come out.

When I opened my eyes the next time, I saw my brother, David's wife and my son Johnny. They were both crying and talking to Matt. I looked for my brother David but he was not there.

Each time I opened my eyes there were different people in my room. At one point David was holding me.

I was going in and out of different machines. They kept poking me with needles and there was so much noise.

I woke up and I felt kind of normal. I tried to move but I had tubes running out of every part of my body. My chest hurt.

I looked around the room. Matt, Dolly, Johnny, Jacob, and Rayen were all in my room as well as my brother David and his wife and my little sister Lucy. Everyone was crying. They were taking turns kissing me on the cheek and they were smudging. I love the smell of sweet grass and the smell was so strong. I felt so much love. I have never, ever felt the love as strongly as I felt in that very moment. The love that surrounded me in that room was indescribable. I tried to speak. I wanted to tell everyone how much I loved them but all I could do was choke. Matt was holding my hand again.

"It's ok Maria we are all here with you. You don't need to fight it anymore. It's ok to let go. We will see you again soon. I love you, my darling. We all love you," and with that Matt broke down crying. I peeked out one more time. I didn't want to go. I wanted to stay here with my family. I started to cry which made me choke even harder. I had just found my family. The light was getting so bright but I wasn't ready and I fought to stay. I opened my eyes and I scanned the room. Everything was so clear now. I stole my one last look, my one last picture. I stole my one last breath. My family was all here together in this room and I finally felt peace. Everything as it should be. The Creator had answered my prayers. I did have my family. I did have my children. All my children.

The light was getting so bright now and I felt so surreal. It was like I was floating. I felt no pain. It would be a long, long time before I would be with my children, my husband, my family again, …for it was time for me to go. I was going home!

I hovered for a brief instant before I left. Don't cry my family. I will see you again.

ROSIE CHRISTIE

17 KATE

I had changed their names. I had shaped their minds. I would always be judge, jury, and executioner. No one had ever stopped me. No one could!

Everyone thought we were just a normal church going, family. They were not aware of the dark secrets we held within the walls of my tiny house by the swamp.

I was the woman with the razor strop and I had made sure every blow connected. When those three little half-breeds finally left I was relieved. I chuckled to myself as I thought back to them.

They didn't even know their own names. I made sure they hated their parents when they left. Oh, I made damn sure of that. I told them constantly whatever I wanted them to believe and they believed it. They were so scared of me. Scared stupid little kids. Well, I wouldn't ever hear from them again. Of that I was sure.

Or at least that's what I thought until the day the sheriff handed me my subpoena. The hair stood up on the back of my neck. Abuse? What? That one-word ringing in my head drowned out anything and everything else that might have been said. I felt I might pass out right there on the step. I kept my composure until he pulled out of the driveway and then my anger quickly exploded into rage.

Those ungrateful little bastards. After everything, I did for them. This was my thanks.

A bolt of straight adrenaline shot through my veins and I grabbed the gun…..

I had instilled the fear of god in them. I am not a woman to be tampered with. How could this be happening?

My one mistake…and I don't make many… was not realizing that these stupid children would grow up.

I knew I should have just killed them when I had the chance. I would have gotten away with it.

ABOUT THE AUTHOR

If you ask me if you ask me if this story is about me, I would have to say, "I can neither confirm nor deny that statement". I love that quote. I have used humor and one-liners for years to help me deal with an unkind world. People are going to speculate and pass judgment regardless of what I say, or write. That is human nature. That is their choice, but my thoughts are as follows, "You Can Judge Me When You Are Perfect."

This book is Fiction – based on true events. Any similarities to any persons or event are entirely coincidental. The abuse suffered by these children, on a daily basis, is a true and accurate reporting and covers a twelve-year period.

I am writing this book because as an abuse survivor I have searched all my life trying to find answers. Trying to find the fix. I have read everything I could get my hands on while it was happening and for many years after. The guilt I felt was consuming. The intense hatred I felt was like a rabid animal gnawing away at me. One thing I do want to make abundantly clear right now is that I never did anything wrong. I was never the reason, nor the problem. There was nothing to fix.

I am writing this for the many children that continue to live in these destructive homes. There is hope!

I am writing this for the many people drifting from one abusive relationship to the next. Don't give up!

I am writing this book to inspire victims. I am sharing the effects of my "Warped Perception" and how abuse has impacted my life in a very negative way. The sequel, "More Than Enough", reveals how Rayen is finally able to turn it around.

There is one message I really want you to think about right now and it is as follows: Whatever you might be going through, past or present, don't allow violence to define who you are! We all have the right to choose. We can choose to let situations eat away at us and entrap us with low self–esteem, pulling us down into depression and addiction so that predators continue to view us as an easy mark. The other option is to choose to be the beautiful people that we were put on this earth to be, that God intended us to be, by lifting ourselves up, lifting others up, staying positive, and surrounding ourselves with inspirational people. Choose wisely.

We can't change anyone else. We need to realize that it is the choice of the abuser to abuse us, and until they choose to stop, they will continue to do so.

I have learned from personal experience, and a few near death experiences, that as much as I love them, I can't fix them. Yes, my heart has been broken, and yes, I have had to walk away many times.

We can't change what has happened to us in the past but we can definitely change our own future. It is not easy, especially if we have been programmed to accept this type of behavior, but it's not impossible. I am fortunate to have a loving supportive family who has helped me along the way but there are many agencies available to you in your area. Don't be ashamed to utilize them.

After leaving home I pushed it as far back as I could and pretended it didn't happen. I used alcohol and drugs as my self-medication, but the use of these products just produced so many other problems. I moved geographically as far away as I could, as soon as I could.

Vengeance was first and foremost in my mind for many, many years and I am thankful I am not sitting in a jail cell. It is all about choices. I made the right one and I am free to write this story.

I have watched alcohol and drugs rip lives and families apart, including my own. I have been blessed with two beautiful daughters, a supportive son-in-law, and one very handsome grandson, whom I love with all my heart. No one can receive the help they need until they ask for it.

Until they are ready. Please ask for help!

It has taken many years but I have learned to look at any situation and find the good. It is not an easy task, but if you look close enough you can find it. As an abused child, my escape was reading. I would read sometimes 3-4 novels a day. The V.C.Andrew's series, "Flowers in the Attic", sticks in my mind, even after all these years. These types of books brought things into perspective for me. I was not alone.

As I pondered what my upbringing had given me I came to the realization that I was blessed with two wonderful gifts.

I had always been an avid reader so it seemed natural to write after I escaped. I had been programmed to NEVER show emotions, speak badly of anyone, say "No" to anyone, or basically, have an opinion at all. Writing transforms me, allowing me to release some of these poisonous thoughts that eat away at me so that I don't act on them.

I was also an avid believer that anyone going to church was a hypocrite and I refused to attend. I felt God like everyone else had abandoned me. I did eventually come to the realization that if not for God, not for attending church every day as a child, having my parents and other family members praying for me, and my guardian angel watching over me I would not be alive today.

Finding God again, was the greatest gift of all and has changed my mind in such a positive way performing miracle after miracle that only our good God can do.

I am a Strong Woman! I am from the Thunderchild First Nation! I am Proud! I am a Warrior!

"It has been said, 'Time heals all wounds.' I do not agree. The wounds remain. In time, the mind, protecting its sanity, covers them with scar tissue and the pain lessens. But it is never gone." --Rose Kennedy